Everybody loves
the Last Kids on Earth series!

"TERRIFYINGLY FUN! Max Brallier's *The Last Kids on Earth* delivers big thrills and even bigger laughs." —JEFF KINNEY, author of the #1 *New York Times* bestseller *Diary of a Wimpy Kid*

★ "A GROSS-OUT GOOD TIME with surprisingly nuanced character development."
—*School Library Journal*, starred review

★ "Classic ACTION-PACKED, monster-fighting fun." —*Kirkus Reviews*, starred review

★ "SNARKY END-OF-THE-WORLD FUN."
—*Publishers Weekly*, starred review

"The likable cast, lots of adventure, and GOOEY, OOZY MONSTER SLIME GALORE keep the pages turning." —*Booklist*

"HILARIOUS and FULL OF HEART." —*Boys' Life*

"This clever mix of black-and-white drawings and vivid prose brings NEW LIFE TO THE LIVING DEAD." —Common Sense Media

Winner of the Texas Bluebonnet Award

THE LAST KIDS ON EARTH

and the MONSTER DIMENSION

MAX BRALLIER & DOUGLAS HOLGATE

VIKING

VIKING

An imprint of Penguin Random House LLC, New York

First published in the United States of America by Viking,
an imprint of Penguin Random House LLC, 2023

Text copyright © 2023 by Max Brallier
Illustrations copyright © 2023 by Douglas Holgate

Visit us online at PenguinRandomHouse.com.

Library of Congress Cataloging-in-Publication Data is available.

ISBN 9780593405253 (Hardcover)

10   9   8   7   6   5   4   3   2   1

ISBN 9780593690741 (International Edition)

10   9   8   7   6   5   4   3   2   1

Printed in the United States of America

WOR

Book design by Jim Hoover
Set in Cosmiqua Com and Carrotflower

For Dana, Leila,

Jim, and Doug.

Thanks, guys.

—M. B.

For Danny Glick

and Church the cat.

My undead companions

during the making of

this book.

—D. H.

chapter one

"You don't have to keep saying that, Jack,"
Dirk groans. "We've been doing 'full speed
ahead, stopping for nothing' for weeks."

"Yeah, who you talking to, duder?" June
says, giving me a little elbow jab.

I shrug. "I'm doing, like, a pirate-captain bit. Why, ya don't like the bit?"

"Not even a bit," June says, smirking. "And what would we possibly stop for?"

"I dunno," I say. "Like if someone needed a bathroom break."

"We're riding on top of a mall containing forty-two bathrooms," Quint points out, very reasonably. "I don't foresee bathroom breaks being necessary."

"Exactly," June says. "We don't need to stop for anything! There is literally nothing in the entire world that would cause us to—"

STOOOOP!

SUDDEN STOP!

MEEP!

We're hurled into our makeshift captain's wheel as the Mallusk screeches to a halt. Imagine a dog sprinting full speed, then suddenly, and with great surprise, reaching the end of its leash. Except in our case, the "dog" is a thirty-nine-ton monster carrying the world's largest shopping mall on its back.

It takes us a moment to gather our senses.

"What happened?" June groans, rubbing at her head.

"Squirrel in the road?" I suggest.

We slowly get to our feet. A tremendous thicket of trees lies ahead of us. Through them, in the far-off distance, we see the reason for the Mallusk's abrupt halt.

An incomprehensibly massive *army* blocks our path forward. An army of skeleton soldiers and evil monsters, called by their master, Thrull. Summoned to the same place we're going: the Tower.

THRULL'S ARMY!

Sorry, hold up, pause.

We need to play a little game of catch-up.

I gotta fill you in on the big important stuff.

First off, the Tower. It's bad news. Once it's complete, it will bring Ŗeżżőcħ the Ancient, Destructor of Worlds, into our dimension.

And Ṛeżžőcħ will do the thing he does so well it's actually part of his name: DESTRUCT THE WORLD. Which basically means devour every living thing on our planet. He's got a big appetite, apparently.

The Tower is Thrull's big project. It was nearly complete, but then he hit a snag. Thrull was missing a crucial piece of information—information that could be gleaned only from the Tower Schematics. And the schematics weren't, like, scribbled on a scrap of paper. They were inside the brain of the monster Ghazt.

So, Thrull snatched Ghazt and brought him to a sentient fortress. Ruling over the fortress was the mad doctor Wracksaw, aided by his loyal Dire Nurses: Debra and Eye-Bulb.

Thrull ordered Wracksaw to open up Ghazt's brain and retrieve the schematics.

My friends and I saw our chance! We'd sneak into the fortress and blow the whole thing up, Death Star–style. Then Thrull would *never* be able to complete the Tower, and Ṛeżżőch would *never* be able to come here. Genius!

Inside the fortress, we made some new friends: the Goon Platoon, a trio of monsters who had undergone cruel experiments and modifications at the hands (tentacles?) of Wracksaw.

The Goon Platoon

Best of all, I found Rover—my monster-dog buddy—who I had feared was lost forever.

That was the good stuff. Everything else was bad.

We *failed*.

Wracksaw probed Ghazt's brain, found the Tower Schematics, and delivered them straight into Thrull's noggin . . .

Also—and this is a big one—Ghazt *died*.
Ghazt was some sort of *monster god*. And when
a monster god dies, a whole lot of energy is
unleashed. Enough energy that the fortress
actually *did* blow up, after all! But, like, a lot
more *up* than we'd planned . . .

The fortress was yanked through a portal and
sent back to the monster dimension. And with
the fortress went Wracksaw, his minions, and
our new pals the Goon Platoon . . .

My friends and I escaped,
thanks to a last-minute rescue by our
buddies Johnny Steve and Skaelka, aboard
the Mallusk.

And Thrull escaped, too. He has everything he needs to complete the Tower and bring Ŗeżżőch to our dimension. But if we can get there in time, maybe we can still find a way to stop it. There must be SOMETHING we can do, right?

So, we're speeding toward the Tower.

Or we were, until . . . we ran into this marching monster-army roadblock.

Thrull's army . . . It's big. Bigger than I ever imagined . . .

At some point, we're gonna have to fight all those dudes, huh?

For the moment, I'm more concerned about how we get around them.

Exactly. Are we supposed to just wait for them to pass? What is this, the evil-skeleton version of *Make Way for Ducklings*?

Apparently, yes: this is the evil-skeleton version of *Make Way for Ducklings*.

You ever try to cross the street during a parade? It's the worst, especially if you're not even there for the parade, because then it's just, like, hundreds of people enjoying the show and you're like, "I JUST WANT TO GET ACROSS THE STREET TO BUY SOME SOCKS! DOES THE SOCK STORE KNOW HOW MUCH BUSINESS THEY'RE LOSING?!"

This is like that, but, y'know—*worse*. Thrull's army seems endless.

But we have our own army! A zombie army! Or, we will . . . *if* I can command them. 'Cause back at the fortress, just before Ghazt kicked the bucket, he did *this* . . .

See me there, clinging to Ghazt's fur? I wasn't having a good time. That same energy eruption that sent the zombies toward the Tower *also* transferred the remaining bits of Ghazt's zombie-controlling powers into my Cosmic Hand. The Cosmic Hand had already been getting weirder, but it immediately got *super* grisly—

Ghazt told me, and I quote, "Now you are the general, Jack."

And then . . . he died.

So, yeah. Lousy timing. Ghazt gave me the power to command *all the zombies*—but didn't tell me *how* to use that power. And I've never been able to control more than a few zombies at a time.

No pressure, right?

A couple of days ago, we passed a big group of
zombies and I eagerly gave my gnarly, souped-up
arm a spin. It was a fail . . .

So now I'm stuck with this gross-out arm
that's supposed to help me lead an army of the
undead—but instead just makes it super hard to
get comfortable at night. And that army of the
undead—it's our biggest weapon in the coming
battle. I need to figure out how to get these
powers to work. And soon . . .

Dirk's voice brings me back to the present evil-army situation. "So, we're stuck, huh?"

"It appears so," Quint says. He's on his toes, leaning over the railing, trying to see where this vile parade ends. There is no end in sight.

"Hey, it's cool," I say, trying *real hard* to stay upbeat. "We'll just wait for them to pass. I mean, really, how big can Thrull's army be?"

So, I guess it's a pretty big army . . .

YES IT IS, JACK!

chapter two

We wait for hours. Then hours stretch into days, and days stretch into a full week. Seven whole days of waiting for this parade of evil monsters to pass.

It's double lousy.

Lousy #1: Let me tell ya—when you're gonna have to battle an evil army, a week of watching that evil army parade past you isn't exactly confidence-inducing.

Lousy #2: We *know* Thrull is close to finishing the Tower. If we want any chance of stopping him, we need to be there, like, *yesterday*. But even if we ditched the Mallusk and went on foot, there's no way past that army . . .

We're in a jam. A jam that has the many monster citizens aboard the Mallusk with us— Malluskians, I call 'em—on edge. Our buddy Johnny Steve, mayor of the mall, keeps trying to come up with fun activities to help everyone relax. But he's like a bad summer-camp director, and his activities are neither relaxing nor fun.

I gotta admit, I'm half-relieved that our journey toward the Tower has been delayed. It's like when you show up for a dentist appointment, then find out the dentist is running two hours behind schedule. Part of you just wants to get it over with, but another part of you is happy for a stay of execution.

'Cause once we get moving again, we'll be at the Tower in no time. And there will be a battle—the BIG battle, for all the marbles. But *what am I supposed to do?*

There's something else that's got me anxious, too. Something that's been gnawing at me ever since we escaped the fortress . . .

Buddy, if we actually succeed . . . If we somehow defeat Thrull and return things to some version of normal . . .

Then it's all over. And then what? Like, my friends go back to school, I guess? Back to their lives. But what do I do?

Yeah, I'm having big emotions.

But I'm not the only one all up in my thoughts.

Quint, June, and Dirk have all been spending time alone, doing serious pondering, too.

What's on their minds? Don't know, no one will spill.

I've learned the hard way that you gotta share the nervous, lousy thoughts that fill your brain. It's like having a crazed puppy in your house. You might not *want* to take that pup on five walks a day—but if it stays cooped up inside, it's gonna tear up your favorite sneakers.

I get it, though. Sharing the hard stuff is . . . hard. It's time for me to give my buddies a nudge.

That night, I find my friends on the deck of the Mallusk. I launch into my best impression of every movie interrogation ever . . .

You're gonna talk! You're gonna spill it all! I've had it with your lips-sealed, secret-y secret feelings-keeping! SO START WITH THE YAPPING!

My friends stare at me, so confused they actually look scared. But it works. And, at once, they blurt out their innermost junk . . .

There are people out there, alive! We saw my parents' names! Quint's parents' names! So where are they?

How are we gonna use Drooler's Ultra-Slime to actually take down the Tower? Filling up Super Soakers isn't gonna be enough.

Ghazt said there would be a Battle of the Tower. But Ghazt also said the Tower will turn on, which means Reżżöch will come to our dimension. So, won't there just be . . . immediate destruction?

And in a flash, Dirk, June, and Quint are firing thoughts back and forth at each other.

Quint says, "I have been pondering the same question as June. We know other humans are alive. So how have we encountered *none of them*?"

June nods vigorously. "I've been watching the broadcast from the survivors. It hasn't changed in months. No new names popping up, no old names going away. So where IS everyone?"

"Where's the *military*?" Dirk asks. He's clearly been bursting at the seams to discuss this topic. "We could use tanks. Tanks could deliver Drooler's Ultra-Slime real good."

Drooler's Ultra-Slime is the one thing that can melt Thrull's vines. Which means it can destroy his skeleton soldiers . . . and maybe even break apart the Tower.

"And like Quint was wondering," June says, "if Reżżóch is gonna show up, how can there even *be* a battle? What does Thrull need that giant army for if Reżżóch is all-powerful?"

I shake my head, bewildered. "Don't know. But Ghazt told me that during the Battle of the Tower, there'd be a moment when a leader could turn the tide. And he seemed to be saying that leader was . . . me."

Everyone is quiet for a second.

"Yeah, we're definitely doomed," Dirk says.

It gets a much-needed laugh. But after that, we're left looking at each other. Guts spilled, questions asked, but no real answers . . .

Suddenly, the mall's PA system screeches and Johnny Steve's voice cries out. *"Citizens of Mallusk City, please remain calm as I inform you that an enemy monster is approaching the Mallusk. RAPIDLY. THAT'S BAD, RIGHT?"*

"Thrull's army," I growl. "Must have spotted us through the trees."

Dirk draws his sword. "Good. I prefer fightin' villains to discussin' feelings." What a poet.

Skaelka bursts out onto the deck. "Weapons up! Remember your training!" she barks. "Combat is upon us!" A throng of Malluskians follows her, tripping over each other and their too-long pj's.

READY!

HEY, CAN I BORROW SOMEONE'S WEAPON? I LEFT MINE IN THE CAN.

THIS IS NOT THE ELITE FIGHTING FORCE I DESERVE.

The PA speakers squeal again, and Johnny Steve calls out: *"I regret to inform you that the intruder has ignored my request to turn back. The perimeter has been breached. I think. Remind me what* perimeter *means?"*

We're all spinning, searching, scanning to spot the intruder.

"Where *is* it?" Dirk mutters.

As if by way of response, I hear crunching and clanging. I rush to the edge of the deck. In the cloudy darkness, I glimpse a figure scaling the Mallusk with shocking quickness.

I jump back just as the figure launches itself over the side.

"THERE!" Skaelka cries. "HIT IT!"

At her command, the Malluskians launch a barrage of mall-made weaponry at the speeding figure.

KRAKA-BOOM!

Their blasts pound the wall—but they miss their target.

When the smoke clears, the creature is darting through the shadows, then, suddenly, leaping over our heads.

"Hang on, Drooler!" Dirk cries, launching himself off an air-conditioning vent.

The sound of steel clanking against armored scales rings out as Dirk's blade harmlessly bounces off the side of the lightning-quick intruder. Again, it's gone, darting and disappearing in the shadows.

I hear the rapid clang of talons behind us. I spin around, but see nothing. This monster seems to be everywhere at once.

"It's impossibly fast," Quint whispers.

At that moment, the creature appears. It has launched itself off a radio antenna, leaping through the air. The deck quakes as it lands with a heavy *SLAM*.

The enemy is silhouetted by the moonlight, leaving only a grayish shape in front of us. I raise the Slicer, readying myself for whatever comes next, when—

"WAIT!" June cries. She takes a slow step forward, looking unsure—then breaks into a sprint, speeding toward the monster . . .

chapter three

Wait . . . June's Winged Wretch buddy? June and Neon are tight like skinny jeans. They went on a wild adventure together, and they share a special, unbreakable bond. Most Winged

Wretches are evil. But not Neon. After their adventure, Neon went his own way, and I wasn't sure we'd ever see him again.

So why is he here now?

June rubs Neon's back, and her hand finds the armor she gifted him. "This barely fits you anymore," she says. "You've gotten so big."

"Oh, wonderful, the enemy intruder is Neon! Hey-ya, Neon!" Johnny Steve calls, waving one of his little wing-arms as he waddles over. "Sorry I told everyone on board to attack you!"

Rover bounds over, playfully shoving his snout into Neon's belly. Neon and Rover met when we first clashed with Rifters. And they made for a super-cute pair, too . . .

June is flopped against Neon, giggling, wiping away tears. I watch their joyful reunion with a little lump in my throat. That nagging feeling hits me again, because this seems like a glimpse of what's to come if we succeed. Endless family reunions and happy tears. That's what everybody wants. What everyone *deserves*. But where does that leave me?

I swallow away my throat lump. I think, *Stop being stupid, Jack. This isn't about you.*

June finally pulls away from Neon, taking his snout into her hands. "Neon . . . I don't understand. How are you here? And why now?"

Grinning like the Cheshire Cat, Neon cranes his neck, reaching for something tucked beneath his armor.

Ooh, I get it. Neon's tracked us down because he needed to bring us some all-important artifact! I wonder what it is? A power gem that will annihilate Thrull? A monkey's paw? An instructional video for leading a zombie army with a weird tentacle hand?

There's a soft, plastic *thunk* as Neon tosses the all-important artifact to the deck, revealing . . .

A very tiny baseball helmet.

OK, wasn't expecting that.

Why is Neon acting like this is some extra-special delivery? I kneel for a closer look, when the helmet suddenly flips over! I tumble back, as—

"Globlet!" my friends and I exclaim.

The sight of our tiny, pink goo-wad friend bursting from the helmet like a snake-in-a-Pringles-can gag causes my heart to leap into my throat.

"Guys!" June exclaims, scooping Globlet up. She's beaming. "Best day ever."

Seriously, what is this—some end-of-the-world reunion special? Is Warg gonna pop out of a birthday cake? Is Biggun hiding in the shadows? Another lump in my throat now. Bardle is the one monster I *really* want to show up—but he never will. Because Thrull killed him . . .

"Globs, we haven't seen you since we left Wakefield," Dirk says. "What are you doing here?"

Globlet waves a hand. "Long story. All I'm gonna say is . . . I will never set foot in a river-boat casino again."

While Globlet begins rattling off all the gossip from Wakefield, I notice Neon nudging the helmet toward June. How many more surprises could fit in there?

June eyes the helmet, curiosity piqued. "Neon, buddy, what little game are you playing?" As June picks up the helmet, I spot the New York Mets logo across the front.

Neon watches June with wide, eager eyes. He reminds me of a dad on Christmas morning watching his kid unwrap that one big gift, waiting for an explosion of joy.

"If this is some all-important artifact that's key to our big quest, well . . ." I say, "it's a little bit out of left field."

No one laughs.

"Left field? Y'know? C'mon, nothing?"
Dirk elbows me, nodding toward June.

"*People?*" I ask. "What people?"
June's voice is barely a whisper. "When
Neon and I were on our own—he was *inside* my
thoughts and memories. He saw what I wanted
most. My family. Other people . . ."

"And I think Neon brought me this to show me he found them. Here," June says, gently tapping the Mets logo.

"Oh yeah, PEOPLE!" Globlet says. "I should have said that right from the start, when I surprise-popped out of the helmet. Yupsies, there are *lots* of people at that stadium place."

It's like the oxygen has been suddenly sucked out of the air. No one says a word. We're too stunned.

People.

"Helloooo?" Globlet says. "Why's no one saying anything? Did I do it wrong? Want me to climb back into the helmet and pop out again? This time I'll say 'people' right away, I swear."

June stands. I see the change pass over her in an instant: reunion over, time to act. "We're going to that stadium," she says. "*Now.*"

chapter four

After that, things happen *fast*.

June and Quint run around like crazed gerbils, charged up at the possibility of finding other people—and, though neither has said it, the possibility of finding their parents.

I still don't know how Neon's going to get us past Thrull's army without being seen, but if Neon sneaked his way in here, he must know a way to sneak back out. We decide the Mallusk—which is incapable of "sneaking" anywhere—will stay put, hidden. Skaelka, Johnny Steve, and our other monster pals will hang back with the Malluskians.

Skaelka grumbles. "I dislike this scheme where you venture out to do big combating while Skaelka is left behind."

As Neon and Rover carry us down the
Mallusk's gangplank, I'm tingling. We might
actually find *people*. But, more than that, the
stadium is in New York City. And so is the Tower.
Everything is pointing in the same direction. At
last, we're going to reach the place we've been
journeying toward for so very long . . .

Soon, we're racing away from the Mallusk, Neon leading us through the remains of the abandoned ski resort. He gallops through overgrown evergreens, running parallel to the marching army while keeping us hidden from view.

From the corner of my eye, I spot a mounted

trail map—and a big "WARNING! DANGER AHEAD!" sign. Seems ominous, but, hey, I'm probably reading too much into it.

I'm waiting to see how Neon will get us past the armed throng when I spot what looks like the mouth of a sewer. Neon leads us toward it. "So *that's* how Neon got to us," I realize. "He used a sewer drain to go *under the army*."

"It's a culvert," Dirk says. "Basic civil engineering, dude."

Whatever it's called, we're going in. Neon carries Quint and June into the tunnel. Dirk, Globlet, and I ride in atop Rover. We're quickly swallowed up by darkness.

The tunnel is pitch-black and seemingly endless. The heavy footfalls of the army tramping above rattle the tunnel—along with my brain and my nerves. It's like racing through a steel drum being hammered on by a giant. Globlet is apparently unbothered—she's snoring.

At last we emerge from the tunnel, and I pull a long gulp of fresh air. My eyes adjust to the sunlight, then I glance back. We've come out a few hundred yards beyond the marching army.

"Hey, we got time for a quick pic—" I start.

"Nope!" June says. "Onward, Neon!"

With that, our breakneck race toward New York begins. Neon's paws pound the ground like a galloping bronco's. The nubs of his severed wings beat like he's trying to take flight, but that won't happen. His wings were sliced off the day the apocalypse began. He's a victim of Ṛeżżǒcħ, just like the rest of us.

We speed through towns and cities that are nearly unrecognizable. Monstrous vines rope around houses, dragging them into the ground. Streets are smashed. Bridges have buckled . . .

As we bound down train tracks, I catch a quick glimpse of Quint. His face is all eager excitement. I get it: he has hope—*real hope*—that he might find his parents.

He's on the highest high, and I'm happy for him. But I'm worried we're heading for the lowest low. We'll soon be at the Tower. And, sure, I'm doing my best to lean into the Cosmic Hand and the monstrous change coming over me. But . . . I still don't know *what to do* when we get there! What happens when the Tower turns on and Ṛeżżőch comes into our dimension?

The frustration and confusion build inside me, until—not even meaning to—I scream, "I JUST WANT ANSWERS!"

"Huh?" Globlet asks, startled awake.

I just want to know how to save us!

Ooooh, gotcha, gotcha. It's too bad Shuggoth isn't here. She knows everything.

I stare at her. "What? Who's Shuggoth? Where is she? Can we ride there, like, *now*?"

Globlet frowns. "No, dodo. Shuggoth's in my dimension."

"OK, not helpful," I say.

"Then *I'm* going back to sleep," Globlet says, curling up in Rover's saddlebag.

"Jack, look," Dirk says, pointing to a battered highway sign. It indicates we're just a few miles from New York City. But even without the sign, it's clear we're getting close. The world practically oozes evil electricity. A faint crackling sound fills the air, and my hair stands on end.

By the time I hop off Rover's back, my legs are rubber, my body is sore, and my nerves are fried. We're nearly there . . .

We round the corner, and there it is. The island of Manhattan stretches out in front of us like an ocean of concrete and metal. Vines cover everything, like a layer of glowing fungus. They wind their way around streetlamps and brownstones, snaking up toward the sky.

I can hear my pulse thudding as I slowly shift my gaze south, toward the Statue of Liberty.

I brace myself, readying my mind for what I'm about to see.

THE TOWER

The sight of the Tower is so overwhelming it practically melts our brains.

June gulps. "This isn't how I—"

"I know," Dirk says. "It's so . . . so—"

"Big," Quint says, his eyeballs glued to the Tower. "Really big."

"And awful . . ." June says. "It's . . . the most horrible thing I've ever seen."

June's right. It's beyond horrible. But . . . I can't look away.

As long and wide as Manhattan is, the Tower is nearly equally tall and thick. It rises up out of the bay like a scorched lightning rod. It's a bleak, ashen thing, built from the rubble of our world. It's shot through with jagged streaks of emerald and magenta, like electric scars. These are vines that Thrull controls—and the vines are the glue that holds the Tower together.

I manage to breathe. I feel like someone ought to say something to mark this moment. But everyone is silent. It falls on me to find the words to commemorate this occasion.

"What?" June asks, staring at me blankly.

"Sorry, first thing that popped into my head," I say. "I meant to be like . . . Guys, we made it. A lot of stuff happened since we left Wakefield, a lot went wrong on the way, but we're here."

"Not sure how to feel about that," Dirk says.

Yeah, tell me about it, Dirk, I think. I'm a jumble of emotions. I feel relief, despite the unknown that awaits. And something like sadness, because, win or lose, our journey is nearing its conclusion. Plus a whole lot of terror, as the Tower seems to pull my gaze toward it . . .

Near its peak, I see something that turns my blood cold: Thrull's throne room. I saw it once before, when I grabbed a fistful of Thrull's vines and experienced a quick, horrible, shadowy vision of the Tower.

At this distance, now, the throne room looks close to microscopic. But that doesn't lessen the terror. It's where Thrull plots and plans to bring Ŗeżżőch—and unstoppable doom—to this dimension.

I can't help but wonder . . . what else does he do up there? I mean, plotting and planning is fun—but it must get old.

Does he, like, take video game breaks between his strategizing-the-end-of-humanity sessions? Do nude aerobics? Perform an intense jumping-jack routine? Does he belt power ballads in the shower?

BABY, BABY, BAY-BEEE YYYYEEEEEoOow!! HEART-ACHE! YAH . . .

I mean . . . who *is* Thrull, really?

I think back to when we first met. When I thought we were actual *friends* . . .

Everything he told us back then was bunk. He deceived me and betrayed me. And after Evie helped bring him back from the brink of death, he killed Bardle—my friend, my mentor.

If Bardle were still here, he could lend some insight into the changes happening to the Cosmic Hand and maybe offer actual answers about how to square off against Ŗeżżőcħ. Thrull didn't only take my friend's life—he removed the only creature in this world able to give us true guidance.

Part of me wants to know more about Thrull. Part of me wants to pay him back for killing Bardle. But the biggest part of me hopes we somehow reach the end of this whole thing, victorious, without ever having to face Thrull again.

"Hey, you coming?" Dirk asks. His voice snaps me out of it.

I see that Neon has paced ahead, along with Quint, June, and a snoozing, loudly snoring Globlet. They're crossing onto the biggest, longest bridge I've ever seen—must be one of those famous ones. It passes high over the stadium.

"Sure, why not," I say. "Only been trying to get here for about a year, right?"

Rover leads the way, guiding me and Dirk onto the bridge. It's jam-packed with long-abandoned cars. We pass taxis with doors hanging half-open. I almost expect some zombified cab driver to pop out.

When we catch up to June and Quint, they're halfway across the bridge. Peering down, we have a clear view into the stadium.

June's gripping the railing so white-knuckle tight that I'm worried it might snap. "I don't see any people . . ." June says. There's a quiver in her voice that she can't hide.

Quint, trying to remain upbeat, says, "But there is certainly *something* afoot down there."

Something's afoot, all right. Instead of perfectly manicured green turf and crisp white baselines, I see torn-up grass and creatures scurrying about. Huge beasts stomp across the infield, pulling massive pieces of machinery. Bizarre mechanisms—not of this world—are being constructed in the outfield.

Those are Rifters. They've turned the stadium into a base. A bigger version of the one where they took me . . .

Ugh, Rifters . . . They're like interdimensional pirates. Zero loyalty. Their only allegiance is to whoever has the most power.

I'm trying to figure out why Neon would bring us to a Rifter base when Dirk says, "Hey, check out the stands."

Squinting, I see that they're filled with glowing spheres, each large enough to fill a seat. I'm about to ask what those spheres are—not like I expect anyone to have a real answer—when I hear the clanging of armor from the far end of the bridge. Then I hear a voice, wet and slimy— just like the creature it comes from—

"Ryḳk?" I manage to choke out. "What's *he* doing here?"

We've dealt with Ryḳk once before. Ryḳk collects things, and I don't mean stickers or comics. He's built a collection of weird, bizarre—and sometimes *living*—things. He took an interest in the Louisville Slicer, so we made a deal. He told us the location of the Tower, and, in exchange, I promised him my blade for his collection—*after* Thrull is defeated.

A shiver runs through my body, and it's not just 'cause I lost track of the seasons and my hoodie isn't cutting it anymore. It has more to do with this series of reunions we've had over the past twenty-four hours—first Neon and Globlet, now Ryḳk—and this unsettling feeling that the Tower is drawing us all here.

I glance behind us. The outbound side of the bridge, where we entered, is clear. There's still a way out. My fight-or-flight is definitely kicking in, and I'm leaning toward *flight*.

But my eyes land on June and Quint. I don't see any "flight" on their faces. Neon brought June here for a reason.

Ryḳk makes a phlegmy whistling sound, snapping my attention back to him. "I caught you!" he says. "Caught you spying on my base."

"Your *base*?" Dirk barks. "Lemme tell ya something. Your 'base' is a sacred site to fans of the New York Mets ball club! It doesn't belong to you!"

Whoa, didn't expect Dirk to get all protective about the Mets. Guess there's something about messing with the American pastime that gets under his skin. Maybe his dad was a fan.

"We're here because . . ." June starts. She swallows. "We think there are people here."

"Ah," Ryḳk says. "You're not wrong. Technically." With that, his armored fist snaps out, smashing into the van beside him. The van topples, revealing one of the spheres behind it. It glows with pink light.

"Have a look-see," Ryḳk says, flashing a cruel grin. He gives the sphere a powerful kick, sending it bouncing down the bridge toward us. It ricochets off an overturned taxi, then rolls to a slow stop in front of us.

Close up, it resembles a giant ball of hardened pink Jell-O.

Quint places his palm against the pink sphere. It gives a little, like pressing your thumb against a rubber bouncy ball. He pushes harder, and we can now glimpse something inside the sphere.

We inch forward, peering closely. And what I see just about knocks the wind out of me . . .

chapter five

Ryķk practically does a little dance, apparently pleased with the way his big reveal went off. He calls, "Oh, relax! The human is alive. When my Rifters open the sphere, she'll wake up, good as new. At least, until Ŗeżżőcħ eats his way through your dimension."

June opens her mouth to respond but then clamps it shut. She glances over the side of the bridge again, peering down at the stadium, confirming what we saw.

"Those spheres!" June shouts, whirling around. "There are *thousands* down there!"

"And each one filled with a person!" Ryķk singsongs. "We've been busy rounding up humans. Thrull wants no one interfering when Ŗeżżőcħ comes."

Quint steps back so he and June and are side by side, shoulders touching. June wraps her hand around Quint's.

"Don't know, don't care!" Rykk says with a dismissive chuckle. "The humans now in the stadium—we found them cowering inside that strange human-lady statue." He waves a hand toward where the Statue of Liberty was, before it became part of the Tower.

Dirk growls. "Is he badmouthin' Lady Liberty?"

Rykk's armor clangs as he plops onto the hood of an old Buick. "But there are oh so many Rifter bases across this land—and each holds oh so many humans."

I watch Quint and June exchange nervous glances. "We don't know for sure they were ever there, June," Quint says. "We just know that they checked in alive from *somewhere*."

June swallows and nods quickly.

"Hey," Dirk says, to June and Quint. "You two OK?"

"The best-case scenario is that my parents are locked inside a giant Jell-O mold," June says coldly. Neon nuzzles her leg. "So, no, not OK."

"Hold up," I call to Ryķk. "You're working with Thrull now? But you told us where the Tower was so we could *defeat* Thrull."

"But we had an understanding," I protest. "Ṛeżżőcħ coming will be bad for everyone in this dimension. And look around, man—you are very much *in this dimension*."

Ryḳk struts toward us. "Thrull has made promises—promises of great rewards! In exchange, my Rifters—and the artillery in our base below—will destroy any who dare interfere with Ṛeżżőcħ's arrival. And Ṛeżżőcħ is coming soon, now that Thrull has the Tower Schematics."

Dirk cracks his knuckles, then sets his big hand on my shoulder. "Hey, Ryḳk. You know Jack's got a whole zombie army backing him up, right? You wanna pick sides? I think you're picking the wrong one. Plus we can combine that artillery you got down there with my little bud Drooler's Ultra-Slime. We can put a real hurtin' on Thrull. Go on, Jack. Tell him."

Dirk squeezes my shoulder so hard my knees just about buckle. Dirk *knows* I can't control an army. But Ryḳk is as slimy as they come—and now feels like the right time to fight slime with slime.

"Yeah," I say. "I control a zombie army. And I'm super good at it. I know exactly how to do it and everything."

"No," Ryḳk says. "I don't think so."

Darn it.

"But . . . you can't trust Thrull!" Quint shouts.

"I trust Thrull more than I trust that this boy can control an army," Ryḳk says. "And without an army, you all will fail. Without an army, my only choice is to continue my alliance with Thrull."

"Forget this," June says. "I'm going down to that stadium. I need to know . . ."

June places a hand on Neon, readying herself to hop on. Quint does the same. But before they can make their move—

In an instant, the Rifters are forming a circle around us.

Ryķk grins. "Like I said, my Rifters will destroy any who dare interfere with Ŗeżżőcħ's arrival. And you all seem like you've got interfering on the brain. So my Rifters are going to take you to the Tower. To Thrull."

The Rifters begin closing in, arrow launchers aimed at our chests.

My mind is racing, trying to think of a way out of this—when one Rifter suddenly freezes. The Rifter's gaze shifts up, looking beyond us, toward the Tower. Another Rifter stops in their tracks, murmuring something.

I feel a chill at my back as I turn to see what's caught their attention.

The Tower has begun to emit an eerie purple glow. A hypercharged hum fills the air.

And I realize . . . it's happening.

Right now.

The Tower is powering on . . .

chapter six

It's what I imagine it'd be like to stand about nineteen feet from a NASA launch, when those big booster rockets ignite—only *cold*. There's no fire or heat—just an icy air, exploding outward from the horrible structure.

A tremendous cracking sound rips through New York City as a million panes of glass all shatter in unison. The rush of icy wind slams into the bridge, rocking it like a hammock in a thunderstorm. For an instant, every abandoned car goes up on its side.

Rover's claws clamp down, puncturing concrete as his teeth snap out to grab me. But my friends and I are already airborne. The blasts rips us off our feet, and Globlet is hurled from Rover's saddlebag, causing her to, at last, wake up . . .

Neon reaches for June, but the wind sends him careening toward an overturned limousine. Ribbons of Ultra-Slime stream off Drooler.

The Rifters—who were surrounding us an instant earlier—are flung fully off the bridge. And we'd be going with them if it weren't for—

"ICE CREAM!" June cries.

SMASH!

The air is knocked out of my chest as I crash into the truck. I flop to the ground, heaving.

I hear Dirk cry, "Look!"

I try to look—but I can't. I can't see anything. For a horrible moment I think that the chill has frozen my eyelids shut. But then I realize my sweatshirt is plastered against my face. The wind is whipping it around, whipping *everything*.

"The Tower is transforming . . ." Quint gasps.

"Guess Thrull finished," Dirk says.

I'm missing everything! I think as I wrestle with my shirt. I finally get a grip on it, yank it down, and—

The monstrous structure is changing. It reminds me of an insect reaching the next stage in its metamorphosis. It rises and swells, like it's doing some horrific version of a morning stretch and yawn. Vines slither and snap as the architecture rearranges itself.

Rover gets one paw around my ankle, and I keep a hand on his head as I stand. The bridge sways more slowly now, as the wind settles.

In awe, Rykk watches the Tower complete its transformation. "Here comes the good part . . ." Rykk says.

I jump back, shielding my eyes as the jagged beam of light streaks upward.

Rykk cackles happily. "The Tower has made its connection with my home dimension. Ṛeżżŏćh's arrival will soon be upon us! Oh, the rewards I will reap! My collection will overflow!"

Suddenly, I feel the Cosmic Hand twist and tighten around my skin. It's practically squirming with urgency. A second later, I realize why . . .

"Uh, guys?" Dirk says. "You seeing this?"

Tiny bursts of color are exploding in the air, like a flea-circus fireworks show. But unlike fireworks, these explosions of color don't fade— they grow. Each expands in the air, forming large, shimmering ovals.

Quint whips his conjurer's cannon from around his back as one blossoms in front of him. He first stares at it—and then stares *into* it. "It's a window into the other dimension," he says. His voice is soft, but there's an excited edge to it.

I don't think it's exciting. I think it's terrifying. We've never glimpsed that world. The closest we've come is seeing Ŗeżżŏch's face, shifting and unformed, back in Wakefield . . .

JACK SULLIVAN. IT IS A PLEASURE TO MEET YOU, FINALLY. DO YOU KNOW WHO I AM?

Ŗeżżŏch the Ancient, Destructor of Worlds.

This is different. This is like someone yanked a zipper and ripped down the fly that separates our two worlds.

I feel a sudden urge to tackle Quint, to stop him from looking into the window. That's the dimension where the monsters came from. Where Ṛeżżőch awoke. Where Ṛeżżőch *is, right now.*

That "tackle my buddy" urge increases when Quint picks up an old plastic bottle and pushes it *into* the glowing oval.

"Don't do that!" I exclaim.

"Why?"

"Just . . . 'cause! Y'know. Or actually, 'cause you *don't* know. Don't poke the . . . rips. Or tears. Or rip-tears. Just don't poke 'em!"

"But, Jack, look!" Quint says, pushing the bottle into the rip-tear again. "These aren't just windows! They're doors."

I swallow. You look through windows. But you can *walk* through doors.

That's what I'm thinking when, as if pulled by a magnet, I'm drawn closer to the rip-tear in front of me. Carefully, like I'm trying to steal a glance at someone else's homework, I peer into it.

For a moment, it's like looking through a busted kaleidoscope—everything is shifting and indecipherable. Then an image slides into focus . . .

I see what looks like a still photograph—a single moment in time. In this frozen moment are creatures in horrible, *forever* agony. Looming over this still, suspended scene are towering, monumental beings. It's like a starting lineup of all-powerful—and, I suspect, all-knowing—bad guys. They stare down at the tormented creatures, uncaring.

I don't understand what I'm looking at. But I can tell it's important. The Cosmic Hand is pulsing and throbbing like mad, and I feel a buzzing in the back of my skull.

Whatever this vision from the monster dimension is showing me . . . could it hold the answer? The answer to the big question that encompasses so many questions: *How do we defeat Ṛeżżőcħ and save our world?*

Ṛeżżőcħ is out there. *Through* there. And according to Ghazt, it's inevitable: he *will* come. With the Tower now powered on, there is absolutely no way to prevent it.

But what am I supposed to do when that happens?

Suddenly, a thought leaps into my mind. My eyes shoot down to Globlet, at my feet. I spit out words rapid-fire. "Shuggoth, right? That's what you said? There's a monster in your world named Shuggoth, and she knows the answers to things?"

Globlet smiles. "A-yup. She knows *all the stuff.* That's her thing. You know, like how your thing is crushing on June but never telling her."

"That is not my thing!" I start, but the whooshing *zip* of an arrow interrupts me. I duck, just in time. The arrow sails past me, vanishing in a blink as it flies *into* the rip-tear.

Glancing back, I see Ryḳk charging toward us, a fresh battalion of Rifters right behind him.

"Seize them!" Ryḳk booms.

"Time to go," Dirk says, hoisting himself atop Rover.

I watch June glance across the bridge, toward the stadium.

She got the answer to her question: *Where are all the people?* But her parents? Their safety? Their location? She's been left hanging . . . This keeps happening. We get an answer to one question, and it always seems to raise another, bigger one. And I'm sick of it. I want *real* answers.

The rip-tear's glowing eyelid-like shape is shutting.

Real answers, I think. *Shuggoth. She knows stuff. All the stuff.*

A dozen feet away, I feel Quint watching me. And in the other direction, June is climbing onto Neon. I lock eyes with Rover, who's ready to start running just as soon as we hop on. His head tilts, confused.

I'll be back, buddies, I think. *Just need to run a quick errand. To the monster dimension. To learn how to save our world.*

My hand tightens around the Slicer. I stare into the rip-tear. "Here goes . . ."

TENTACLE!

The tentacle bursts through the rip-tear, stabbing into our dimension! Before I can react, the tentacle has ensnared me, curling around my body like a slime-soaked lasso.

Globlet makes a "wheee!" sound as she's knocked off me. The Slicer falls from my hand. I lunge for it, but I miss. Because I'm being ripped off my feet and dragged, headlong, into the rip-tear . . .

I can't believe it.

I may have just uttered my last words—and they were *Here goes tentacle . . .*

chapter seven

As I'm dragged through the rip-tear, I half-
expect to see something like that cockpit
view of the *Millennium Falcon* blasting into
hyperspeed—a million tiny pinpricks of light all
suddenly stretching into infinity.

But I don't.

And to my happy surprise, I don't see the
tentacle either—it's vanished.

What I do see is so much worse.

I see *myself*, tumbling through cosmic
nothingness. It's like I'm watching myself on-
screen in real time. This out-of-body weirdness
turns into an out-of-body nightmare as, from
my disembodied view, I see my arms and my legs
and my torso begin to stretch . . .

You know when you chew up a huge wad of bubble gum, grab it, and stretch to see how far it can go? Well, it turns out that me and gum have more in common than I thought, 'cause that's what's happening.

Finally, when my noodle-y limbs can stretch no farther, I watch my body *explode* into pieces.

I want to reach into this tornado and grab every piece of ME I can. It's like that carnival game where some sucker stands in a glass booth while cash whirls around them, trying to grab as much as they can in thirty seconds.

Only here? I'm the sucker *and* I'm the cash. I can't grab anything, because my arms are out there, floating around in the abyss.

But if every part of me is in pieces, how am I even thinking right now? How am I conscious? *Am* I conscious? WHAT DOES ALL OF THIS MEAN? I can feel my brain-scrambling panic spike, and then my mind, mercifully, seems to shut down. It can't handle what's happening right now—and so it won't. Instead, I find myself thinking about what I saw moments before . . .

Quint's face, just before I stepped through the rip-tear. My best friend—the first *real* friend I ever had—watching me walk into the unknown.

I wonder if that's the last time I'll ever see him. I wonder if that's the last time I'll ever see *anything*.

A faint, distant voice causes my eyelids to snap open, like window shades yanked too hard. Which means: woo-hoo, I have eyelids! And my other body parts, too! I'm in free fall, tumbling though cosmic nothingness, toward a pinprick of light that's rapidly growing as I plummet toward it.

I hear the voice again. It's calling, "I got him! I got him!"

Suddenly, an explosion of colors and then . . .

FLOOP!

I'm in . . . a net. I kick and thrash in confusion. My hands thrust out, pawing at the netting, pulling myself upright. And then I see . . .

Wait. What??

The net splits, and I flop to the floor like a fifty-pound tuna. On the ol' scale of confusion, I'm somewhere around a billion. Less confused than when my body was bubble gum—but only barely.

"It's OK. You're home, buddy," Dave says soothingly. "Now give us a hug."

"This is not his home!" Peaches barks.

"Home is where the hugs are," Dave says. "You're safe now."

"He is *not* safe," Peaches says. "Stop telling lies!"

"I'm trying to ease him into this," Dave whispers. "Remember how scrambled our brains were after we got sucked through?"

Peaches scowls. "Your brain is always scrambled, Dave."

"What are you guys *doing* here?" I ask. My own words sound faint and distant, like I'm underwater. Great. On top of everything else, my ears are all plugged up. I try yawning. No luck.

"We're here to rescue you," Cannonhead Johnson grunts. "Caught up to ya just in time."

That's when I realize: we're *moving*. Everything is bucking and swaying. Wind stings my cheeks. A wet-dog odor comes from somewhere. I follow the smell to the trembling deck beneath my feet.

"Mamooph," Dave says, apparently indicating the creature we're riding.

Suddenly, Cannonhead whirls, swinging a hunk of artillery the size of a refrigerator. "Strayfurs are back! TIME FOR MORE FUN!" he barks, lifting and firing the cannon.

BOOM!

Well, that *BOOM* did it—popped the ol' eardrums, and I can hear again. And what I hear is . . . combat.

I turn to see what Cannonhead was firing at—but I can't pinpoint it, because there's *so much* to fire at.

Yep, Peaches was right. I'm not safe at all . . .

Great. I survived an interdimensional tumble only to land directly in the middle of the monster version of *The Fast and the Furious*. The flurry of action finally knocks me out of my portal-tumbling daze, and suddenly my senses are firing at full force.

Lightning crashes, slicing sideways through a red sky. I glimpse huge, shadowy beasts on the horizon. A geyser erupts, and a shrill, ghastly shriek follows.

"Y'know what . . ." I say, trying to sound calm as I glance around. "I think I'm gonna, maybe . . . yep, I'm just gonna hop back through the nearest rip-tear thing. I'm pretty sure I left, um . . . the stove on. At home. In my dimension. So, yeah—anyone see one of those rip-tears I could just jump through real quick?"

"Ah, bummer, no," Dave says. "They only opened for a moment, when the Tower powered on."

Suddenly, metal flashes and one of Peaches' blade-arms stabs into my sweatshirt. "Get to cover, human!" she barks, hurling me across the deck of whatever huge beast we're riding atop.

"HEY!" I shout, about to tell her to watch the hoodie, 'cause I didn't think to bring an extra on my interdimensional journey. But I smash into a railing, the wind goes out of me, and it's all I can do not to barf over the side.

Beneath us, I see a river flowing with a thick, magenta liquid. In the far distance, I see gargantuan monsters, unmoving, bodies rotting in the sun like a fleet of beached whales. I suspect that carcasses of Godzilla-sized creatures aren't a regular feature of the landscape. I'd like to ask what happened to them, but I have more immediate concerns . . .

The monsters swarming around us—strayfurs, apparently—make me think of mutant hornets, built in a laboratory. Whirling rotor blades sprout from their backs, like those little helicopter seeds that fall from trees in the summer. Stubby stinger-tails fire energy-charged needles.

The strayfurs fill the sky, like one big swooping, sweeping blur. I'm so busy avoiding the needles pounding the deck that I don't even notice the snarling strayfur zipping low toward me . . . until it *slams* into me, taking me right off my feet. My heels bump and stutter against the floor as the thing pushes me across the deck, pincers snapping . . .

Whirlybird
rotor wings

I grab the pincer closest to my eyeball—figure
I should take care of that one first—and wrench
it sideways. The strayfur lets out a gurgling
cawww sound, opens its mouth to bite into my
face, and then—

There's a wet *splat* as a hundred flying slugs
slam into the creature, blasting it away.

I turn to see Cannonhead Johnson, the slug-
firing cannon on his head still smoking.

"You owe me," he starts to say, but then one
heavy shot explodes against the deck, sending
all of us staggering into a wall, momentarily
hidden beneath an overhang.

"Could everyone just be cool for one second and tell me what's going on?" I shout. "Who are we fighting?!"

Peaches looks past me. I follow her gaze—and get my answer.

Wracksaw.

He swoops into view, his bulbous frame aloft in midair, atop the most stomach-churning strayfur yet. Wracksaw has changed since I last saw him. The mad scientist bobbing in front of me now looks almost like he was broken, then rebuilt. Overhauled, remodeled—made more monstrous.

chapter eight

I lock eyes with the monster who killed Ghazt. Who tried to kill me and my friends—but failed. Who tried to deliver the Tower Schematics to Thrull—and succeeded.

His demanding, bossy whine splits the air. "SEIZE THE BOY WITH THE COSMIC HAND!"

I glance around the deck, hoping to find some other kid with a Cosmic Hand. No luck.

Wracksaw roars, "He's standing right there, looking confused! Seize him, Debra-Bulb! The one with the hand!"

"Hey!" I shout. "We've *all* got hands!"

"Not me," Peaches says, tapping her goo-splattered sword.

"Fine," I mutter. Then I shout again, "We've all got hands except for Peaches!"

Then . . . wait . . . what did he say?

Wracksaw has two Dire Nurse minions: Debra and Eye-Bulb. But he just said *Debra-Bulb*, like they're a single entity. Maybe 'cause Wracksaw's so self-obsessed that he can't be bothered to differentiate between them? Or maybe because—

I shriek in revulsion as Debra and Eye-Bulb swing into view. At the same time. Atop the same strayfur. Because Debra and Eye-Bulb are now . . .

It's like they've been smushed together—
jammed and collided and rearranged. I wonder
if their shocking synthesis is a side effect
of passing through Ghazt's portal? Or is it
more of Wracksaw's horrible handiwork? I
could definitely see him Frankensteining his
subordinates to unleash a little rage.

But right now, it doesn't matter how they
turned into this. What matters is that they're
seconds from steering their strayfur into me and
plucking me off the deck.

"Seizing the boy, sir!" Eye-Bulb shouts.

"That's what I was gonna say!" Debra shoots
back. "WRACKSAW, SIR, WE ARE SEIZING
THE BOY!"

"Don't copy me!" Eye-Bulb snaps. He turns to
scowl at Debra, causing the strayfur to suddenly
swing to the right. Debra shrieks, the strayfur
caws, and a massive needle attack is unleashed.

BOOM!

A dozen sparking shards pound the
Mamooph's hide. It lets out a pained, angry
grunt and stampedes faster, putting some
distance between us and the bad guys—if only
for a moment.

With a second to breathe, I grab the Goon

Platoon for a quick huddle-up. "Here's the deal," I say, forcing myself to sound at least a tiny bit confident and competent. "These rip-tears opened, and I saw—well, I dunno, exactly. Like, awful *beings* looming over something even *more* awful. But whatever I saw—I think it holds the key to how to defeat Ŗeżżőcħ. And my buddy Globlet told me—"

They all gasp.

"Globlet the Infamous?" Peaches asks.

"Globlet the Charming Rogue?" Cannonhead Johnson asks.

"Globlet the Late-Night Queen?" Dave asks.

"What? No. Different Globlet. Globlet the, uh, sassy, maybe. Doesn't matter, she's still in my dimension. But she told me there's a monster here who knows, like, everything—and can hopefully decipher what I saw. A monster named Shuggoth—"

At the word *Shuggoth*, the Goon Platoon gets weird. Even though it's quick, I catch it: Peaches shooting Dave a glare, like a warning. But Dave ignores it.

"Shuggoth knows just about everything, that's true," Dave says. "But to speak with her, you'll need to—"

Peaches slams the dull side of her blade against his mouth, silencing him. "No. It is risky."

"The kid stepped through a dimensional wormhole and straight into a battle with Wracksaw," Dave protests, pushing the blade away. "*That* is risky."

"Risky for *him* alone," Peaches says. "A consultation with Shuggoth would endanger many."

Peaches and Dave stare at each other a long moment. A stalemate.

It's Cannonhead Johnson—the last of the trio I'd expect to help me—who breaks the silence. "The little dude will die just trying to *reach* Shuggoth. And the little dude kinda bugs me, so I don't really care. I'll tell him. Shuggoth's at the Hidden City."

"Wait, I bug you? Why do I bug you? Is there one specific thing or—" I start, then pause, realizing Cannonhead just gave me Shuggoth's location! "The Hidden City! Got it, good, finally making some progress. Geez—it's like pulling teeth with you guys."

"Ooh, pulling teeth!" Peaches exclaims. "*That* is my preferred rainy-day activity! Forget

Shuggoth. Stay here with us, and we will play pulling-teeth games. First game begins now!"

No thank you . . .

I'm about to ask the Goon Platoon a few more questions: Can they hook me up with a ride to the Hidden City? What makes talking with Shuggoth so risky? Should I bring Shuggoth a gift or something, like a loaf of banana bread?

But I don't get the chance.

The sky is draped over by a huge shadow. I

look up. It's not storm clouds, not a solar eclipse, not a misplaced patio umbrella.

It's hundreds and hundreds of strayfurs buzzing through the air. And leading them, front and center . . . is Debra-Bulb.

From somewhere, I hear Wracksaw bark, "Just GET HIM!"

A boom splits the air as Debra-Bulb's strayfur unleashes an energy-charged needle barrage. The glowing artillery arcs through the sky and then—

The deck *explodes*.

I'm suddenly airborne—flipping, whirling, end over end. I feel like the showdown wheel on *The Price Is Right*. With each rotation, I catch a glimpse of the attack's aftermath—

Debra-Bulb, their strayfur's tail-cannon leaking fiery steam.

The Mamooph, barreling ahead.

The Mamooph deck, aflame, no more Goon Platoon in sight.

Then, suddenly . . . a violent jerk!

Two of them, actually.

The first violent jerk is a wrenching tug as one of Wracksaw's armacles snatches me, *yanking* me toward him.

The second violent jerk is Wracksaw.

He just is.

"The passage between dimensions was not easy on my already enhanced and modified body," Wracksaw says. "Much damage was done. And it left me . . . grotesque!"

"Y'know, you weren't exactly easy on the eyes before," I say. "This might be an improvement."

"Oh, it *is* an improvement!" he says with a crazed smile. "Grotesque is good! The damage offered opportunities to alter my anatomy in new, exciting, and wonderfully repulsive ways . . ."

This mad monster has me in his grasp and could end my life in an instant—but I can't help it; I have to bite back a laugh. I mean, c'mon—he sounds like some sort of deranged toy commercial . . .

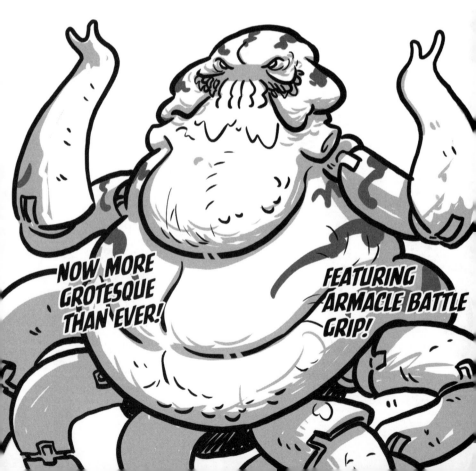

NOW MORE GROTESQUE THAN EVER!

FEATURING ARMACLE BATTLE GRIP!

Wracksaw's shrill, screw-loose cackle snaps me back to the present. "But the PAIN . . . I will pay you back for *that*." With one armacle, he taps the Cosmic Hand. "You are undergoing alterations as well," he says. "As I said you would . . ."

I think back to what Wracksaw told me in his fortress . . .

YOUR MONSTROUS TRANSFORMATION IS NOT INEVITABLE. I COULD REMOVE THE COSMIC HAND. THAT IS WITHIN MY CAPABILITIES.

"You considered my offer," Wracksaw says. "You should have accepted. Because now you have no choice: I will remove that foul appendage. I will not be gentle. And I think I'll make a few alterations while I'm at it. Like I told you: you'll be one of us, soon enough."

I swallow hard. This weirdo really knows how to strike at the spots where I'm most vulnerable. What if I came all this way, I actually get the answers I need . . . but I return home as some half monster, while my friends continue on with their lives? Wracksaw's vile threat causes a fresh spike of fear—what happens next, when this is all over—

But a flash of movement behind Wracksaw interrupts that train of thought, thankfully.

Wracksaw sniffs at me. "Oh, is that fear I smell?"

"Nope," I say, starting to smile. "That's Dave."

Wracksaw twists, just in time to see Dave leaping at him. "JACK IS FINE! HE'S LEANING INTO IT!"

Dave lands on Wracksaw like a wrestler launched off the ropes. Wracksaw lurches. Dave starts pummeling, and Wracksaw yelps in pain. His armacle goes slack, and I'm released.

Falling. Again.

There's a sound like a cracking bullwhip as the armacle snaps out, trying to recapture me. It hits my cheek with a sharp sting, but my free fall continues.

Wracksaw, grunting and gasping as he grapples with Dave, roars, "Pray you do not survive this fall, Jack Sullivan! I promised you pain, and I will not break that promise. But I will break *you*. I will follow you to the ends of this dimension . . ."

Wracksaw's mad ranting trails off as the world below rushes up at me, fast.

My only hope is that this dimension is so wildly different from mine that, I dunno, the ground is made of, like, Wonder Bread. That's what I'm imagining—soft, chewy, pillowy bread—when—

CRACK!

Not Wonder Bread, I think, and everything goes black.

chapter nine

Time has passed. Not sure how long.

I blink open my eyes and see a blur of colors. I paw at my face, and my hands come away covered in some strange, half-liquid goo, like melted fruit snacks. And I feel something wet on my lips . . .

STAY WITH ME, JACK! YOU'RE GOING TO BE OK!

Wait, Globlet? Globlet's here?! And she's . . . attempting mouth-to-mouth resuscitation?

"Globlet, I'm OK!" I say, managing to sit up and pull her away from my lips.

She shimmies off my chest. "We kissed!"

I wipe the back of my hand over my mouth. "You taste like Twizzlers." I spit out another stream of goo and glance around. We're on a raft, floating down a bubbling, rainbow-colored river. "Globlet! How are you here? What's going on?"

"You landed in this river. We pulled you onto our nifty raft. Then I saved your life and you acted like a regular Wendy Peppercorn about it."

"I'm not a regular Wendy—wait . . . *we*?"

At that moment, I feel a tap on my shoulder.

"Geez-Louise, talk about making a fella feel unwelcome," Globlet says. She pats Quint's hand.

"That's not what I meant . . ." I start. "But—"

"I couldn't let you go through that rip-tear alone, Jack," Quint tells me. "So, I followed you."

"And I got stuck to his jacket, like lint!" Globlet says. She sounds very proud to be like lint.

I shake my head. "Quint! That was dumb!"

But no matter how angry I try to sound, I can't help but feel relieved. There have been a lot of times I've been happy to see Quint, but this tops them all.

At the same time . . . this complicates things. What if Globlet was wrong about this Shuggoth creature? I mean, I wouldn't trust Globlet to keep the class hamster alive for the weekend, yet somehow I've traveled to the monster dimension on her advice. If Shuggoth can't help us, then my stroll through the rip-tear hasn't just possibly stranded *me* here—but Quint, too.

I shake away those thoughts and get down to business. "Guys, in that rip-tear I saw . . . something bad. But it's like . . . I don't know the words to describe it."

"Ooh, I love this game." Globlet taps her chin. "OK, I'll go first: Person, place, or thing?"

"I don't know!" I say, suddenly feeling very

tired. "Place? Thing? Monster? The last stop at the end of the universe? All of the above. No idea! It was . . . vague and fluctuating horror. But the Cosmic Hand started throbbing, and I felt like, whatever I was looking at . . . it was the key. That's why I stepped through."

"Ahem. '*Stepped* through'?" Globlet repeats. "You were yanked through by a tentacle! Kicking and screaming and sobbing and there was snot coming out of your nose! We saw. Don't pretend you did a big brave leap."

"I was *about* to step through! And I wasn't sobbing with snot and whatever!" I exclaim. "Look, if this Shuggoth monster can decipher what I saw, I think I'll know the answer to the big question: HOW TO STOP ṚEŻŻÕCĦ."

Quint looks at me for a second. Did he glimpse that same horrifying nightmare?

After a long moment, he says, "Odd. I saw nothing like that."

I swallow. Great. Now it feels like what I saw was shown to *me*, specifically, for a reason.

But *what* did I see? Was it the future? The past? Some really jacked-up monster dimension fast-food joint? I need to know!

I glance down at the Cosmic Hand, remembering the way it tingled and pulsed.

That's when I first really take note of our raft—and realize it's not a rubber dinghy or one of those lazy river inner tubes. It's the rotted, bloated corpse of a monster.

"Well," Quint says. "Now that we're all together, it's time we meet with Shuggoth. Globlet, lead the way!"

Globlet smiles timidly. "So . . . about that. I don't actually know *where* Shuggoth is." She glances at me, then quickly whispers to Quint. "Jack's gonna get real mad now, huh?"

"Nope," I say, "not at all. 'Cause *I* know where Shuggoth is. Guess who I saw here?"

Quint thinks for a moment, then says, "Chet Brophy."

"Wait . . . huh?" I ask.

"Chet Brophy," Quint says. "From homeroom."

"Why would I have seen Chet Brophy from homeroom in another dimension?"

Quint shrugs. "You told me to guess."

Globlet leans forward, chin on her hands. "Soooo . . . What did Chet Brophy have to say?"

"I DIDN'T SEE CHET BROPHY!" I exclaim. "I saw the Goon Platoon."

"You did?! I'm jealous," Quint says. "How are they?"

"I didn't ask."

"Rude!" Globlet says.

"Um, there wasn't exactly a lot of time to catch up! They grabbed me right when I came through the rip-tear."

Then I tell Quint and Globlet everything that happened after I landed: the strayfurs, Debra-Bulb, Wracksaw promising to inflict untold pain on me. And I finish with the biggest thing: "Shuggoth is in the Hidden City."

"Then to the Hidden City we'll go!" Quint says.

I just hope this Shuggoth doesn't require a blood sacrifice or something as payment for her services. Also, Cannonhead said we'd *die* trying to get to her, which doesn't sound great. But none of those thoughts are gonna help things, so I say, "Globlet, lead the way."

Globlet hops to her feet. "NOT A PROBLEM! Is what I would say if I knew where the Hidden City was. But I don't. Never heard of it."

I stare at Globlet. She gives my arm a chummy little jab. "*Now* you're gonna be real mad, huh?"

OK, yep, I am officially freaking out. We have a destination—but no idea *where that place is*!

And somehow I'm the only one who seems to think that's *bad*! Neither Quint nor Globlet seems particularly concerned about *anything*. I mean, Quint is currently eyeing a piece of fruit dangling from a tree limb, whispering something about how perfect the color is. Globlet is trying to blow the biggest bubble ever.

Guys! Can we please FOCUS!

I hang on to Quint until the fruit finally comes off its branch, sling-shotting us back into the corpse-raft's bloated gut. Then I pop Globlet's bubble with a jab of my finger, and she flops onto the raft, covered in gum.

"Great," she mutters, plucking at strands of purple gum, like this is the biggest concern of the day.

I look from Quint to Globlet, then back to Quint. *What's the matter with these two?*

"Um . . . guys?" I start, planning to remain calm—but quickly feeling that plan fall overboard. "THIS IS SERIOUS! I SAW A HORRIBLE NIGHTMARE-SCAPE! It *might, maybe, possibly* be the key to saving our dimension. We need to talk to Shuggoth. BUT WE DON'T KNOW HOW TO GET TO SHUGGOTH!"

Quint stuffs the fruit into his bag, then looks up at me with a contented, carefree smile. "Jack, it's going to be OK," he says. "I just have a feeling."

I can't believe it. Usually *I'm* the upbeat, fake-confident one! What's happening here?

"You're all Mr. Science and Logic, but now you're suddenly A-OK with everything because of . . . what? A hunch?"

"Bingo!"

Before I can question that further, a stream of gooey liquid erupts from one of Corpsey's eyeballs, blasting me right in the mouth.

"Oh goody," I sigh, wiping my face. "Our raft has sprung a leak."

There's no response from Quint or Globlet, and I see Quint's carefree smile has changed to a look of intrigued confusion. He's ogling at something behind me. I turn and see—

"A waterfall," I gasp.

The river is carrying us toward the base. But, wait . . . There isn't any liquid raining down. I squint. Something is off about the whole thing. Like I'm looking at an optical illusion that I can't quite solve.

At the bottom—or top?—of the *watervault*, the river is funneled upward in a towering tornado of swirling liquid.

"Incredible . . ." Quint says, again awestruck by the realities of this dimension. The astonished look in his eyes when he saw the fruit, and now the watervault—this place is like one big playground for Quint. A very hazardous playground full of freaky monsters, inconceivable terrain, and never-ending danger. And he wouldn't even be here if I hadn't gone through first.

We have to get to Shuggoth, and fast—before Quint decides to become a permanent resident.

The river picks up speed, dragging our corpse-raft over jagged detritus, ever closer to the watervault. Waves of syrupy liquid splash over us. The monster dimension's strange atmosphere collides with the river, and I smell something like Fruity Pebbles and burnt hair being sucked into the torrent of liquid.

"Hold on! Corpsey's taking us for a ride!" Globlet cries out, clinging to the corpse-raft with her hands—and a little help from all that bubble gum.

And then we're rocketed upward, brain-rattlingly hard. It's like we're riding the Tower of Terror in reverse—and the brakes just exploded. I grab handfuls of the corpse-raft's loose, putrid skin, desperately clinging to it as we're thrust higher and higher.

My stomach flips endlessly.

I keep my teeth clenched grizzly-bear tight, just in case my guts turn inside out and try to escape. We finally reach the watervault's peak—but the raft keeps going, momentum hurtling us skyward. I scream my head off as the raft spins and spins and spins . . .

We hang in midair for an impossibly long moment, then splash down. And it's a *long* way down. When we hit the river, goopy liquid rains down on us, pummeling the raft. It sounds like cannon fire.

But we're alive. It takes me a while to believe it, but soon, the current carries us to calmer waters. Finally, I feel safe enough to lift my head. And gasp.

chapter ten

The sprawling structure in front of me leaves
me speechless. At least, I *hope* it's the sprawling
structure that has me speechless and I didn't
swallow my tongue during our not-nearly-as-
fun-as-it-sounds reverse waterfall ride.

"Welcome to Port Teekay," Globlet says.

Quint sits up, eyes bright. "Now, *this*," he says, "looks like the place to find someone who knows where the Hidden City is."

"Even better," Globlet says. "We can grab a taxi that will take us there!" She elbows me. "See, Jack? And you were being a big ol' worrywart."

I nod, breathing a massive sigh of relief. Quint was right—he said it would all work out, and it seems like maybe it will. If we find someone who will take us to the Hidden City, then we could get answers from Shuggoth and be heading back to our dimension in time for dessert.

Corpsey carries us beneath arcing bridges that look like long tongues, bending and twisting at impossible angles. A bird-monster as big as a jumbo jet swoops over us, carrying a creature-packed gondola, settling in for a soft landing. Smaller airships rise from behind the port's walls, jetting off, headed to who knows where. I count a dozen more watervaults, all of them spitting ships out into the wide harbor.

Port Teekay is like an airport as imagined by someone with a 109-degree fever, and Quint is loving it. "Jack," he says, tapping my arm excitedly, his eyes as wide as Frisbees. "We are in . . . another dimension!"

I'm struggling to wrap my head around
Quint's new supercharged, super-enthusiastic
explorer attitude. He continues to show *zero*
fear or concern about *any of this*. And—despite
my *infinity* fear and concern about *all of this*—
his excitement is starting to rub off on me . . .

"You're totally right," I say, grinning. "Dude, no human has *ever* done anything like this before."

"We're like Neil Armstrong and Buzz Aldrin," Quint says.

"And the other guy," I add. "Was it Tom Hanks? I think it was Tom Hanks."

"The other guy *wishes* he was Tom Hanks," Globlet says. "And don't get me started on Neil Armstrong. He's the guy that was, like, *super proud* just 'cause he took one small step, right? We've taken a *ton* of small steps, and you don't see me yakkin' about it."

Quint ignores us. He's too busy looking around, taking it all in. "What a startling variety of vessels!" he says.

The churning liquid carries a jaw-dropping array of boats and rafts and ship-creatures. We're the only ones riding atop a dead monster. But hey, maybe that's a good thing? I mean, we gotta look pretty intimidating right now. All those times I showed up for the first day at some new school? If I had arrived on a dead monster, I probably would have gotten pushed around a lot less . . .

But as the boats all begin to converge, nearing the dock, I see a *lot* of creatures eyeing us, and none of them look particularly intimated by our craft. Guess I had that one wrong.

"We're drawing a lot of attention here, guys," I say. "And with Wracksaw chasing us, we need attention like we need a hole in the head."

Our attempt at docking only draws more attention. The other vessels slow, gently dropping anchor. But not us! Our leaky corpse-raft plows straight into the dock with all the subtlety and grace of a rhinoceros diving into a pool.

We're flung forward, toppling hard onto the ground.

I throw a quick glance at Corpsey, half on the dock, half-submerged. We need to get going, fast, and not draw any more attention.

Unfortunately, Quint slips on corpse goo, falls, stands, then falls again. "WHO LEFT THAT THERE!" he shouts. "IT'S A REAL SAFETY HAZARD!"

Real helpful, Quint.

Globlet flicks Quint's knee as we finally make our way into the throng of monsters ahead. "Hey, bozos, pipe down! Can't ya just be cool?"

Quint thinks that over. "It would require a lot of effort," he concludes. "And would still likely be unsuccessful."

Globlet harrumphs, like we're a lost cause. We're passing a booth that sells sunglasses, and Globlet snags three pairs. She throws on a pair of incognito shades like she's too cool for this dimension, and then hands the others to me and Quint.

"These sunglasses have six lenses," I say.

"Mine have eight," Quint says happily, like it's a contest.

"No doy, that's the point," Globlet says. "Wracksaw's trying to find you, Jack. You and Quint are the only two humans in this entire dimension. So, you need to look like you belong here—blend in."

"Wouldn't *paying* for the sunglasses help us

blend in better?" I ask, but before Globlet can answer we're plunged into a crowd exiting the port's main terminal, and Quint shows off his uncanny ability to blend in . . .

I yank Quint away before we get flattened by the crowd. Hundreds of monsters slither, stomp, and slide through the doors, doors big enough to accommodate monsters as tall as houses.

"We can take a taxi up here," Globlet says, waving us onward.

We turn a corner—and my sunglasses are nearly whipped off my head. An endless stream of taxis zips past us, speeding down a road so full of loops and curves it puts most roller coasters to shame. The taxis are a blur of spikes and tails and ground-quaking hooves.

"Hey, Globlet, are there any taxis that don't look like they'll eat us?" I ask. But I don't get an answer, because Globlet is already dashing off, quickly disappearing into the crowd. "Be right back!" she shouts. I frown. Probably spotted a creature selling discount bubble gum remover.

"Do not fret," Quint says cheerfully. "We'll hail a taxi ourselves, then find Globlet. She'll see that we can blend in with the best of them!"

Without hesitation, Quint sticks a thumb out into the street to get a driver's attention. We get a lot of weird looks. What if sticking your thumb out is, like, a really obscene gesture in this dimension? I don't want some bruiser of a taxi driver breaking or liquefying or blasting off our thumbs. I like my thumbs! And June and I have an endless game of thumb war going, and we're tied at 247–247. If I get back home with a melted thumb, my hopes of winning are shot.

I'm looking around when I spot the most bizarre taxi yet. Parked halfway on the curb is a *hand*. It looks like Thing from *The Addams Family* was zapped with a giganto ray.

I look for the driver—but instead, I see two tiny pink feet sticking out from underneath . . .

She's underneath the taxi, like a mechanic working on an old junk-box car. But this is a *living creature*. What's she doing? Rewiring its finger-intestines? Tinkering with its palm-brain?

Head spinning, I reach down, grab her little pink ankles, and yank her out. I half-expect to see her covered in grease, but nope—just a bunch of crumbs and some empty candy wrappers.

"Oh, hi, Jack. What's up?"

"We're supposed to be finding someone to drive us to the Hidden City!" I say, trying to stay calm. "We don't have time for your . . . tomfoolery."

I just said *tomfoolery*. I've never said *tomfoolery* in my life. See, this whole adventure is frying my brain.

"Quiet!" Globlet says. "You wanna alert the enforcers?"

"Yeah, Jack, you wanna alert the enforcers?" Quint says, coming around the taxi. "Hey, Globlet, what are enforcers?"

"WAIT! Globlet, are you—?" I kneel down, whispering. "Are you *stealing* this taxi?"

"*Helloooo*, did you not hear me? I said, 'We can *take* a taxi up here.' What did you think I meant?"

"Globlet!" I say. "You *cannot* steal a taxi!"

"No, I totally can. I'm doing it right now," Globlet says. "Why are you all dumb now, Jack? Do you want to save your dimension or not? I don't think the answer is 'not,' so I'm stealing this. I just gotta get the taxi to like us—so I'm feeding her yummy sweet treats."

"But—" I start.

"Don't feel bad about it," Globlet says. She waves in the direction of a disheveled monster, asleep at a table covered in meat scraps. "This taxi here is starving, while her driver there is passed out in a food coma."

"But you don't even know how to get where we're going!" I say.

Globlet sighs. "Dude, it has GPS. C'mon! Now make yourself useful and stand lookout."

After a few minutes of lookout duty—where most of the looks are directed at us—I whisper to Globlet, "What's the status? How we lookin'?"

She peeks her head out. "Like dorks," she says, then slides back underneath.

Just then, a throaty, wet voice barks, "Does that belong to you?"

The crowd parts to reveal a tall, wiry monster who's all weird angles. She wears a uniform that shimmers in the light, like it's made of unicorn hide. I spot a very intimidating utility belt around the monster's waist—each pouch is a fanged mouth. One drips saliva.

Oh crud, I think. *This must be one of those enforcers Globlet mentioned. She wants to know if this is our taxi. And this is very much* not *our taxi!*

The enforcer raises one long arm and points toward the dock, where our deflated corpse-raft is slowly sliding into the water.

Oh, our raft. OK, phew—that's better than getting busted for stealing a monster vehicle. Unless using a deceased monster as a raft and then abandoning it at a busy transit hub is considered *worse*—which, now that I think about it, sure sounds a lot more heinous.

I give Quint a sideways glance. We need to keep this enforcer busy while Globlet finishes up feeding time with the taxi. So I do my best to defuse the situation—with a big ol' lie . . .

"That was our best friend," I say. "And we're pretty broken up about what happened to him."

"*That* was your best friend?" the enforcer asks. We all turn our heads to watch liquid bubble up as our corpse-raft—I mean, our best friend—slowly sides off the dock, flops into the water, and sinks.

"That's the one," I say, weakly.

"He died as he lived," Quint says. "Wetly?"

The enforcer stares at us, trying to get a read on just how full of garbage we are. Apparently, she thinks we are very full of garbage—because red and blue beams suddenly erupt from her eyes, cascading down our bodies.

I wince, thinking we're gonna be disintegrated or melted. But fortunately these aren't, like, deadly laser beams . . .

The lights finally flicker away, and the enforcer says flatly, "Scan complete. Initiating database search. Analyzing . . . Processing . . ."

I gulp. She's totally about to discover we're not from this dimension. I don't know exactly how bad that is—but if word gets around, it won't be hard for Wracksaw to find us.

Just then, Globlet pops out from beneath the taxi. "All set, guys! This baby—who I've named Seabiscuit, BTW—is ours. So let's—"

Globlet freezes, noticing the enforcer.

In turn, the enforcer sees Globlet. There's no scanning needed—Globlet is instantly recognized. And I get the sense they're not old pals.

"Starburst M. Globlet . . ." the enforcer says. "I have been looking for you for a long time."

Globlet looks at the enforcer, and then . . .

YOU'LL NEVER TAKE ME ALIVE!

chapter eleven

The enforcer starts to take a step forward,
but her body jerks and jitters. She's still in
the middle of analyzing me and Quint, and
apparently she's not great at doing two things at
once. Fair enough. I can never do the "pat your
head and rub your belly at the same time" thing,
and doing some sorta identi-scan while trying to
grab Globlet looks a lot harder.

Thinking back to all those old Westerns Dirk
made us watch back in the tree house, I put on
a country drawl, tip a nonexistent cowboy hat,
and back away slowly. "It's been a pleasure,
ma'am, but it's time for us to be getting along
now."

That's when the identi-scan finishes. A twitch runs through her body, like a warning signal. Then her eyes flash and—

ALERT! OTHER-DIMENSIONAL CREATURES DETECTED! ENFORCERS ENGAGE!

The enforcer barks, "SET PHASERS TO STUN—"

Hey, stun? That's not too bad. I figured she was gonna say "incinerate" or something.

"STUNNINGLY PAINFUL!" she finishes.

Oh. Darn.

"It's called a getaway! Not a stayput!" Globlet shouts, shoving her face through the open taxi door. "So let's gooooo."

Quint scales the taxi's long fingers, and I scramble up behind him. The fingers are in desperate need of some lotion, and we use the rough skin like a ladder. I jam my foot into a callus the size of a basketball, use a knuckle as a final handhold, and hoist myself inside.

I expect to find Globlet flipping switches, powering up engines, checking coordinates. Instead, she's sitting calmly in the middle seat, slurping a drink the size of a football.

I want to ask her a *lot* of questions—most of them some variation on "WHY ARE YOU WANTED BY THE MONSTER POLICE?" But for some reason, the question that pops out of my mouth is . . .

Suddenly, Seabiscuit stands, and everything sways. I'm thrown into a fleshy armrest, then go flipping over a fleshy cupholder, and when I'm finally upright again, I'm sitting in the also-fleshy driver's seat.

"Oh, good, I was hoping you'd want to drive," Globlet says, hopping up front. "My footises can't reach the scale-pedals."

Actually, no, I *don't* want to, but I see the enforcer's glowing eye-beams shining into the cabin. And a trio of enforcers is on the road ahead, marching toward us. It's pretty clear I've got no choice.

"Drive . . . Right, OK," I say, searching for the ignition or a button or *something*. "And I do that . . . how?"

"You do it . . ." Globlet says. "With gusto!"

Globlet grabs a long shard of bone that pokes through the cabin floor. It's like a gearshift, I realize, as Globlet pushes it forward. There's a squelching sound—then Seabiscuit lurches forward, swinging around, charging *into* the terminal.

"Wrong direction!" I shout. "This is a getaway. That means we're supposed to be *getting away*!"

"Fantastic!" Quint remarks. "I was hoping we'd get to see inside of the terminal during our tour."

"IT'S NOT A TOUR!" I cry as I desperately jerk the wheel back and forth, trying—and mostly failing—to avoid hitting anything.

Seabiscuit gallops past landing platforms and heaps of wreckage and endless shops and stalls and emporiums.

"Ooh, Pinky Palace," Globlet says, pointing. "That place has the best sammiches."

"We should stop for some," Quint says.

"If you two don't get serious, I WILL PULL THIS CAR OVER!" I roar. "Actually, I won't, 'cause I don't know how to and also 'cause we're being chased by an army of monster police. But, yeah . . . GET SERIOUS."

Globlet glances back at Quint, and they both giggle. I want to strangle them. I suddenly feel very guilty about every time I horsed around in the back of some tired parent's car as they drove me home for car pool.

Seabiscuit skids around a corner, swerving into a wide corridor. "A way out!" I say, pointing at a huge, arcing exit up ahead. I can see the daylight beyond.

But much of that daylight disappears as enforcers begin to fill the opening. First three or four, and then a dozen of the glow-eyed monsters. They ride beasts, nightmarish mash-ups of machinery and musculature.

The enforcers and their beasts move closer, forming a roadblock. And we're racing straight toward it.

One enforcer tosses a snake creature into the path ahead of us. All along its back, its scales erupt into spikes—spikes that will shred Seabiscuit's finger-feet if we drive over them.

I quickly scan our surroundings, looking for another way.

"Just go, man!" Globlet says, tugging the bone-shift and hurtling Seabiscuit forward at runaway-freight-train speed. Meanwhile, Quint just stares out the window in fascination. "Look!" he exclaims, tapping the glass. "A remarkable time-telling device!"

The enforcer stands front and center at the roadblock, looking supremely confident. But I see that confidence start to fade as Seabiscuit continues barreling ahead, fingers stabbing the ground like jackhammers, cracking the floor.

"They are not stopping!" one enforcer shouts.

I kiss my fingertips and touch the ceiling. I saw it in a movie once and thought it looked cool. Plus, when will I get to drive a stolen hand-taxi again? Hopefully, never.

I shut my eyes, bracing myself for the coming crash.

But there is no crash. Instead, I feel my stomach flipping. I open my eyes, and see—

We hit the ground with a jarring, jerking *thud*—dipping low, then springing back up as Seabiscuit's fingers flex. Stunned, I twist around to see that we've cleared the roadblock.

The enforcers attempt to follow us, but they're thwarted by their own roadblock, all the creatures jammed together, slamming into one another. They're climbing out of their vehicles, shouting at one another.

Seabiscuit swerves out onto the road, galloping away from the port. "We just barely escaped!" I say, letting out a breath. I allow myself to enjoy our moment of success. "And Just Barely Escaping is my middle name."

Globlet turns to me. "Shut up! It is?! That's amazeballs. I'm learning so much about you guys! My middle name is Marge."

For about a quarter of a second, things feel OK. Sure, we're in the monster dimension, but things could be worse! We could be—

"Hey, look—it's us!" Quint exclaims. "Giant, in the sky! We're famous!"

"We're wanted," Globlet says, sounding half-annoyed and half-honored. "That's a wanted alert."

"Oh," Quint answers, processing. "Oh, dear."

I gulp. Yep, things are worse. We're wanted by
Wracksaw, Debra-Bulb, and every other creature
in the monster dimension . . .

chapter twelve

We just pulled off an epic getaway from the monster-dimension police, and it feels like victory—but only for a moment.

Not only are Wracksaw and his minions after us, but those enforcers put a bounty on our heads. The entire *dimension* is hunting us. Although, apparently, that's nothing new for our little pink friend . . .

"Globlet, you are a serious CRIMINAL in this dimension?" I exclaim. Though, honestly, I'm only about 81 percent shocked by this revelation.

"I'm not a *serious* criminal!" she says. "I'm a jokey criminal. I steal from the rich and give to—"

"The poor?" I ask, hopefully.

"No. I give to the rich, too. It confuses *everyone!*"

"Your rap sheet was pretty extensive," Quint notes, proceeding to recite from memory everything on Globlet's WANTED alert . . .

WANTED! DIABOLICAL CRIMINAL MASTERMIND

✗ Identity Theft of the Nameless One

✗ Mowing a Public Lawn Without Prior Authorization

✗ Selling Counterfeit Countertops

✗ Using a Child's Kite as a Getaway Vehicle

✗ Cheating at Monopoly (Řežžőch Edition)

✗ Refusing to Apologize for Cheating at Monopoly (All Editions)

✗ Daring Daylight Robbery in the Realm of Endless Darkness

✗ DJing Without a License

✗ Scratching and Sniffing Scratch 'N' Sniff Stickers Prior
to Purchase

✗ Claiming, Without Evidence, to Have Invented the Word *Funky*

✗ Misrepresenting Self as a Small-Town Lawyer with a Heart
of Gold

✗ Tooting in a Crowded Room

✗ Ruining 219 Surprise Parties

✗ Planning and Organizing a Complex Jewelry Heist,
then Oversleeping on Day of Heist

As admittedly fascinating as Globlet's criminal history is, we've got to keep our eyes on the prize: Shuggoth and the Hidden City.

Globlet reaches for the taxi's GPS—which is actually a brain in a jar—and turns a dial. A map begins to grow, spreading out across the windshield like frost on a cold day. Words flash, and Globlet harrumphs. "Hidden City not found," the map says before it disappears.

Before I can react to this latest setback, there's a loud *ZAP* and Quint shrieks.

I spin around. In the back seat, Quint is waving one hand in the air, blowing on it. "All is well!" he says. "Just a minor shock."

Something is laid out on his lap, in pieces— he's been tinkering with it. Quint tinkering is nothing new, but my heart sinks when I realize what this is: his conjurer's cannon. Quint's cannon is a powerful tool, which gives him, like, real-deal wizard powers. It lets him wield monster-dimension science—which, to us, looks a whole lot like magic.

"What happened?" I ask, eyeing the dismantled weapon. It takes him a long moment to answer.

"Technically—" Globlet starts to say, but Quint shoots her a look, and she zips her lips. He must be pretty upset about his busted cannon—or embarrassed.

"Hey, it's OK. I dropped the Slicer when that tentacle grabbed me," I say. "We journey into another dimension, we both drop our weapons. Great heroes, huh?"

"The cannon will work again," Quint says confidently.

I hope he's right. It's clear we're gonna need all the help we can get to make it to the Hidden City. And that's *if* we can find it. Which—without GPS—is again feeling nearly impossible. It's not as if we can just pull over and ask someone where it is since, y'know, we're wanted criminals.

"GOT IT!" Globlet says.

Huh? I turn back to find Globlet hanging off the dashboard, gnawing at the GPS brain with her teeth. The brain swirls in the jar, changing colors, and the map spreads across the windshield again. This time, there's a big blinking symbol in the upper-right corner.

"There ya go," Globlet says, tapping the glass. "Hidden City."

"But—how did—?"

"You don't get the name Globlet the Shortcut Shorty without hacking the occasional GPS," Globlet says, strutting proudly across the dash. "It's not gonna be a cupcake walk, though . . ."

She begins pointing to other symbols on the map, listing the many obstacles we're likely to encounter. "Death pit. Snake pit. Peach pit. Dead Guy Gulch. Desert of Eighty-Seven Sinkholes. The Weird River Crossing. And worst of all is this stretch here," she says. "A full day's journey—with *no bathrooms*."

"So, what are we waiting for?" Quint asks, leaning forward and flashing me an enthusiastic double thumbs-up. OK, then. The path is perilous, but we have a destination. And it feels good.

"Just hop on that speed pass up there, and we can get this party started," Globlet says, pointing to a barely visible road beyond a glowing, hairy guardrail.

I nudge the bone-shift, and Seabiscuit jerks back, rearing up on two fingers, like a cockroach just skittered past.

Globlet groans. "I said hop, Jack. HOP. Y'know, like, *jump*."

My eyeballs roll so hard I can actually feel them scraping against the sockets. "I thought this was the monster dimension, not the *super-literal* dimension," I mutter, then tug the bone-shift up and shove it forward in one herky-jerky movement.

"Thatta boy!" Globlet cries as Seabiscuit *pounces* like a cat trying to catch a laser pointer's glowing dot. Seabiscuit vaults over the guardrail and hits the ground running, which is fortunate, because—

It's a mad-dash race through the monster dimension. We travel roads like half-pipes, full of white-knuckle turns and loops and drops. Off-ramps materialize out of thin air, plunging us down new, impossible-to-predict pathways.

For the first few hours, I'm not sure I even breathe. I'm too busy dodging bands of wheelie-popping skeletal bikers, avoiding being run off the road by aggressive taxi-creatures, and trying not to get flattened by centipede trucks as big as cruise ships.

Making matters worse, Globlet is just about the world's lousiest copilot. She found an old *Monster* magazine in the glove box, and now she's slumped in her seat, feet on the dash, grumbling about the "Slurpiest Man Alive" award being totally rigged. Occasionally she looks up to say, "Jack, you missed the exit. Again."

Finally, I just about explode. "Globlet . . ." I say, teeth clenched. "I've never driven a hand-taxi. I've never driven in this dimension. And I've *definitely* never driven a hand-taxi in this dimension. In fact, I'm thirteen years old—I'm not supposed to be driving anything anywhere!"

"Yikes, you are old. GROSS," she says, then quickly points. "Take that exit, 10,901.121 and a half! Right by the comically oversized roadside tooth. Not the regular-sized tooth. THE BIG ONE."

"That exit just looks like one big hole in the ground!" I protest, even as I'm jerking the wheel, veering across thirteen lanes, cutting off a swarm of very tiny vehicles, and then almost losing my lunch as we plummet downward. Then everything flips and we're rocketing upward, spit out into some entirely new region of this world. Everything here is metallic and sparkly, like a nuclear glitter bomb exploded and no one bothered to clean it up.

"What is *that*?" Quint asks, excited. I glance out the window and see an enormous cockroach-looking monster lying on its side, wings blocking the sun. Dozens of smaller creatures dine in its shadow. Servers ride around on roller skates. The cockroach yawns.

"Brunch," Globlet says with a shrug.

"How incredible . . ." Quint murmurs. He's hanging on to Globlet's every word, and she's eating it up. Soon, she's in full-on tour-guide mode, like a super-enthusiastic history teacher leading her class's field trip to the museum.

Behind me, Quint is frozen in awe. I'm determined to *not* get overwhelmed by this brain-scrambling world, so I keep my hands tight on the wheel and my eyes glued to the road. If we're going to reach Shuggoth, I can't get distracted by the endless bizarre sites, strange landmarks, and towering advertisements.

That last one, though—the advertisements?
That proves to be a problem, 'cause I fail to
realize that the billboards are actually alive,
and—

As we speed away from the very hungry billboard, Quint lets out a long-held breath. "Well, that almost turned our *first* ride across this dimension into our *last* ride."

The words *last ride* remind me how much this feels like a sort of grand finale. One last ultimate adventure, me and my best buddy. And if it is . . . maybe I should try a little harder to "lean into" this, too.

"OOH OOH OOH!" Globlet exclaims. "There's Connie's, just ahead! I once chugged a whole truckload of blueberry bile there! We gotta pull over for a pic!"

Globlet shoves her hands *into* her belly, digs around, and pulls out . . .

"Hey!" I say. "That's *my* camera!"

"Duh, it is. I grabbed it from your room on the Mallusk. I used to borrow it all the time back in Wakefield, before you guys *ditched me* for your big road trip."

Globlet taps the camera's screen, bringing up a hidden folder. She swipes through dozens of pics—photos of all of us back in the day, when times were simpler. Well, simpler, as apocalypses go.

Globlet the Kodak Bandit, I think, as we pull over to pose for a pic . . .

If it were up to me, we'd stop only for emergen-
cies. And you'd think it *would* be up to me, since
I'm the one driving this claw cab. But it's not.
Globlet's the one who freed Seabiscuit, so now
the pair is all buddy-buddy. All she has to do is
toss a piece of food through the floor and let it
bounce into Seabiscuit's "mouth," and she pulls
right over.

Which means there's *a lot* of pulling over. Quint can't go thirty seconds without spotting some bizarre rest stop he wants to check out or some roadside attraction he *must* retrieve a souvenir from. And I don't protest as much as I probably should, because it's all amazing. An other-dimensional quest turns even the most mundane pit stops into mind-blowing excursions. Like . . .

Stopping to stretch . . .
–IN THE MONSTER DIMENSION!–

A quick fill-up . . .
-IN THE MONSTER DIMENSION!-

The farther we drive, the more I notice monsters eyeing us suspiciously. Then it hits me: we haven't seen any other hand-taxi monsters. If we're the only ones, it won't be hard for Wracksaw or the enforcers to find us. Luckily, Globlet knows a guy who knows a guy who can make any vehicle unrecognizable. I figure *that* is worth a stop. Although, I figure wrong . . .

Speeding away from Rudy's Rest Stop and Refuse Ranch, we hit a long stretch that's nothing but bad news. Decomposing husks of monstrous vehicles litter the road, reminding me of the abandoned cars in New York. Buildings are half-melted, like heaps of ice cream on a warm day. They cry out as we pass, and I'm reminded of what Skaelka told me: many buildings in their world are alive.

"Oh no . . ." Globlet says quietly. "When Ŗeżżőch awoke from his slumber, he really jacked up my world . . ."

She stares out in silence for a long while, then lies down on the seat. She puts her sleep mask on—but I don't think it's nap time. She just can't look anymore.

I never gave a ton of thought to what happened to this dimension when Ŗeżżőch awoke. I know lots of monsters were ripped from this world and flung into ours. But I now realize Ŗeżżőch unleashed a lot of havoc here, too.

Back home, right now, basically every living human is imprisoned in an orb. My friends are maybe safe, but I don't know; I can only hope. And the Goon Platoon? Last I saw of 'em, Dave was dangling from Wracksaw, and Peaches and

Cannonhead Johnson were . . . hopefully not blown up by the same blast that threw me off the Mamooph.

All that terror and pain is a result of Ŗeżżőcħ and his vile servants.

We *must* defeat Ŗeżżőcħ before his servants hurt anyone else. We *must* stop him before he comes to our world and destroys everything.

I grit my teeth and nudge the bone-shift forward, pushing Seabiscuit faster toward the Hidden City . . .

chapter thirteen

When I first hear the sound, I assume it's just a ringing in my ears—a result of Quint teaching Globlet how to play slapjack, a game she has some trouble understanding . . .

But the buzzing sound builds toward cacophonous as we drive, and I realize it's something much worse than Globlet face slaps. "Strayfurs," I snarl.

The road curves, and suddenly we're bearing down on hundreds of stopped vehicles. A monster traffic jam.

I jerk the bone-shift back. Seabiscuit clamps down, halting so quick that Globlet is flung from her seat. She smashes into the window with a *SCHPLOOT*, clings to it for a moment like a sticky hand, and then plops onto the dashboard.

"Globlet, take the wheel," I say as she stands, eyes spinning like a cartoon character's.

"No problem!" she says, hopping over.

I yank the wheel from her and jam it back into place. I stand up in my seat, poking my head through the open roof. Looking out, I see trucks like giant, mutated caterpillars. Caravans of hollowed-out carapaces. None of them moving. Then I see why . . .

"Debra-Bulb . . ." I say.

Quint squints. "Incredibly horrific," he notes.

I nod, biting my lip as I watch Debra-Bulb and their gang of strayfurs search every vehicle that passes through their blockade.

Debra-Bulb barks out orders. It's faint, but I hear something about *the boy* and *the hand*.

"How did they know we'd be going this way?" I wonder nervously. I'm trying not to let myself get hijacked by frustration or fear.

Globlet timidly plucks gum from her leg. "Whoops. That may have been a Globlet Goof."

The strayfurs are buzzing low, examining each vehicle. Some draw a closer look from Debra-Bulb. And when I watch Debra-Bulb tear another car in half and begin interrogating the occupants, my mind is made up.

"We need to get off this road," I say, turning the wheel. "We'll wait until dark. Hopefully we can sneak past then."

———————

Moments later, I'm steering Seabiscuit through a field of furry grass as high as a basketball hoop. I'm hoping it's tall enough to keep us tucked away if Debra-Bulb does a flyby.

Seabiscuit is happy to give her fingers a rest, finding a small mound and plopping down atop it. She must fall asleep right away, because soon the taxi is gently bobbing and swaying.

Globlet is next to drift into dreamland. She removes a mouth guard from her belly—something I *really* want to question—and curls up. Soon, spit bubbles are dripping from her mouth.

I want to stay alert, because who knows what brain-splittingly bizarre new threat might pop up next. But I feel a nap coming on—the type you can't beat.

In the back seat, Quint's tinkering with the conjurer's cannon, and the sound is oddly soothing. I'm drifting off to sleep when I hear Quint whisper, "Jack, guess what? We're having a sleepover in another dimension."

I blink my eyes open, smiling. "You're right. Dude, life got pretty weird, huh?"

"Indeed, friend."

At the end of the world, in a monster-zombie apocalypse, you end up catching zzz's in a lot of weird spots. Junkyards, classrooms, shopping malls. It's like an endless string of strange sleepovers. My favorite, though, was the first night after Quint and I reunited. Forty-three days after the Monster Apocalypse began.

We made Mr. Goodbar s'mores, then stayed up until two a.m. playing Mario Kart and talking and laughing about anything and everything.

That was my favorite, because that's when it felt like everything might actually be OK.

Now, though . . . it feels like nothing is OK. Whatever I glimpsed through that rip-tear, it's like it's burrowed up into me, shooting me full of doubt that was never there before. And the last thing I saw before leaving our dimension was the Tower powering on. What I saw through the rip-tear was horrifying—but I don't know what it means. I know what the Tower powering on means, though: we're close to the end . . .

Somehow, despite all of that, Quint's more hopeful than ever.

And if this is our last hurrah, the final quest before the big showdown—I'm gonna do my best to follow his lead.

"Sorry your cannon broke, buddy."

Quint lets out a quick chuckle. "It's all right. After all, sometimes you need to break something before it can be improved."

I glance down at my arm. At the Cosmic Hand—which, in a lot of ways, felt like it broke *me*. And continues to scare the bejesus out of me. But maybe Quint's right . . .

"If the world hadn't broken," I say, "we wouldn't be here."

"I don't think it was worth it," Quint says, laughing quietly. "But . . . "

I nod. I know what he means. And then . . . I'm fast asleep.

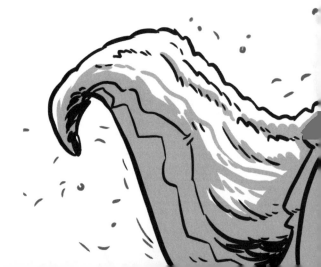

chapter fourteen

Movement jostles me awake.

The first thing I notice: the sound of the strayfurs and Debra-Bulb is gone. *Whew.*

The second thing I notice . . . The ground is moving? Or we're moving? *Something* is moving. I glance out the window, and—

But my friends are already very awake. In the back seat, Quint and Globlet are playing something like checkers—using glowing fingers as pieces.

"What the—? What's happening?" I ask.

"You parked on top of a clumberthod," Globlet says, like I should have known that. She kicks back, leaning against a pile of overflowing bags. It would seem Quint accumulated A LOT of souvenirs while I was snoozing.

"Yay for happy accidents, right?" Quint says, right before he slams a finger down onto the board. "And for *another* happy victory."

Globlet smacks the board. "I am losing VERY SORELY RIGHT NOW!"

"Uh, guys?" I start, trying to dial them back in. "How is this a happy accident?"

"Well," Quint says, "the clumberthod got us right past Debra-Bulb's roadblock."

"Oh. That is good," I say. My wake-up panic is starting to settle down. "How long have we been on top of this guy?"

Globlet grins. "Long enough for us to learn a *ton* about you. You talk in your sleep. Lots of stuff about Pop-Tarts, cheat codes, and June—"

"OK!" I exclaim. "Why didn't you wake me up?"

Quint shrugs. "You seemed comfy."

Something in the distance gets Globlet's attention, and she suddenly hops to her feet. "We're nearing the crossing," she says, crawling into the passenger seat. "A river we'll need to pass to reach the Hidden City. The clumberthod won't take us much farther."

In the distance, I see a shadowy canyon.
I have zero idea how I'm supposed to drive
our taxi down—and off—this massive, loping
monster. But Globlet simply tosses a bag of candy
out the window, and Seabiscuit follows, leaping
to the ground below.

"Good-bye, new pal!" Globlet calls to the
clumberthod. "I hope we'll keep in touch! I'll
write! But you have to write first!"

As soon as the giant creature is out of earshot,
Globlet spins around—

chapter fifteen

"The crossing is just through here," Globlet announces cheerfully.

Right. Just through the shadow-drenched, spooky-as-a-late-night-walk-to-the-bathroom canyon. *Yay*, I think as I swallow and urge Seabiscuit forward . . .

The canyon walls stretch up, staggeringly tall, allowing almost no light in. The darkness seems to swallow us. If not for the otherworldly sounds and smells, this place could have been yanked straight from one of Dirk's favorite Westerns.

And, not for the first time, I think about Dirk. And June. And Rover. I miss them. But, weirdly, I'm sorta happy they're not here. Beside me, Quint's doing long division under his breath as he works to repair his conjurer's cannon. And there's something that feels right about it being just the two of us, in this dimension, on this journey.

But that doesn't stop me from worrying about our pals. A lot. "Quint," I say. "Dirk and June . . . you think they're . . . y'know?"

"I *meant*," I say with a sigh, "do you think they're *safe*?"

"Oh, without a doubt," Quint says, smiling. And it seems like he should be more worried than he is, given that we're a full dimension away and all, but, I dunno . . . I want to believe him.

"HELLO! DUH!" Globlet says. "Obviously they're OK. They know how to take care of themselves *way* better than you do. June makes you guys look like a pair of butt cheeks."

"Like, each of us is a pair of butt cheeks?" I ask. "Or we're each one cheek on the same butt?"

QUINT

Two cheeks, same butt. You're the right cheek.

JACK

Lefties are known to be smarter.

That's when I spot the first flickering light, high above us. Squinting, I can just make out small structures affixed to the wall. Another flicker of light gives me another glimpse: they're dwellings, cobbled together from scavenged junk.

"Let's pick up the pace, huh, Seabiscuit?" I say.

As we travel deeper into the canyon, my guts start to feel like they're floating, unattached, inside my belly—flipping and rolling as Seabiscuit carries us over the rough ground.

Then Seabiscuit's steps become softer, as though she's gliding, moving across the ground like a puck on an air-hockey table. Glancing down, I notice one of my shoelaces is loose—and the end is drifting upward, waving about like a tiny flag.

This place is strange, strange, strange . . . I'm thinking, when Globlet suddenly points. "We made it!" Globlet says. "The Weird River Crossing!"

Far ahead, the semidarkness gives way to a stunning array of light, rising up and stretching out. Colors I've never seen. Like one of those majestic renderings of space you see in science-class books.

This, I realize, is the point where the canyon ends, all land stops, and the river crossing begins. I'm about to give Seabiscuit a final nudge, when a thin, tinny voice calls out—

"THE CROSSING BELONGS TO US!"

Two small creatures spring up, clambering onto a small mound at the end of the canyon. Squinting, I see that they resemble little gremlins. One is green and shiny; the other is purple and basketball-shaped.

Quint shoots me a glance, rubbing his chin. "I believe we may be facing a classic troll-bridge scenario."

"But with really small trolls," I add.

"We're not trolls! We're gorblins! I am Flustrod," the first creature says. "And this is Pillksort."

Quint stands, poking his head through our taxi's open sunroof. He gives the pair a big, too-friendly wave.

"Greetings, Pillksort and Flustrod," Quint calls in a voice that is equally too friendly, considering how troll-bridge encounters always seem to play out in stories. "Would I be accurate in assuming you will now present us with a riddle? And if we answer correctly, we may pass to the crossing beyond?"

The two gorblins exchange glances. A pause, then Flustrod says, "Yes . . . A riddle!"

"Of course there is a riddle. Obviously," Pillksort adds. Then, a little quieter, "Tell us, though, what's a riddle? We know. We just want to make sure *you* know."

I frown. OK, these are not riddle-trolls. Not trolls at all. So then what do these tiny "gorblins" want from us?

Globlet leans in. "I dated a gorblin once. It got weird. Kept trying to take me on dates to Worm Wrestling matches. They're *super* into fighting."

"The small pink ball is correct!" Pillksort calls. "We enjoy nothing more than the sights and sounds of combat!"

Flustrod says, "Any who wish to pass must fight! And the losers have left behind a very extensive collection of blood-splattered armor!" A metallic clang rings out as Flustrod's pointed tail stabs at the pile below him.

They're standing on a heap of armor, I realize, my stomach churning. I look up at the junk-made dwellings on the canyon walls again. "Guys," I whisper. "These gorblins must ambush poor, unwitting travelers and sucker them into some sort of battle to the death."

"*We* are poor, unwitting travelers," Quint says, like this is another happy accident.

"And easily suckered!" Globlet adds, proudly.

"NO WHISPERING! ONLY FIGHTING," Flustrod calls, his tail stabbing out toward me and then Quint. "YOU WILL FIGHT!"

Quint shoots me a glance. We hold an awkward smile for an uncomfortably long moment.

"You won't be fighting *each other*," Pillksort says. "Just ONE of you will do the battle dance with our undead beastie, STARGROVE."

Wait, did they just say *undead*? They have . . . a zombie monster? Or . . . a monster zombie? Would that be a mombie? Or a zonster? No, those sound dumb. Some new word that—

Quint is suddenly poking me excitedly. "Jack! This is new information! We know the zombie plague *came* from this dimension, but we've only witnessed its effect on humans. We've never seen a *zombified monster*."

I nod. The idea of such a thing never crossed my mind. Never thought about it, never saw one—and I have zero interest in seeing one now.

"Hey, uh . . . y'know what, gorblins, never mind," I say. "We'll pass."

"No, you won't!" Pillksort shouts. "Didn't you hear anything we said? You don't pass unless you fight!"

OK, my bad, that bit of confusion is on me. "I meant, *pass*, like we'll *skip* on the whole—"

"NO SKIPPING! ATTEMPTING TO CROSS THE RIVER VIA SKIPPING LEADS TO DEATH," Flustrod barks. "JUST ASK BOGARTH THE SKIPPING WARRIOR. OH WAIT, YOU CAN'T, HE'S DEAD."

I groan. "We're not doing your little fight thing!" I call. "Keep your lousy river crossing. We've changed our mind—"

"Don't believe ya, big top-dog liar!" Pillksort yells.

"I'm not a big top-dog—"

Flustrod shouts, "SHOW US STARGROVE! SHOW US . . . THE BATTLEBALL."

At that moment, beams of light slice through the darkness. I see that a large section of the nearest canyon wall has been dug out and carved away, creating a sort of huge, open, circular cave.

At the center, floating gently, is a round cage. It's also built from scavenged material and looks like it must weigh three tons—but somehow, it bobs in the air. A spine-chilling chittering sound fills the canyon as *hundreds* of gorblins begin descending from the structures above us. Some rappel down on ropes of snakes. Others simply walk down the canyon walls, looking like a bunch of suction-cup-shoe aficionados headed to a big meetup.

I now realize why this whole place feels so weird and wrong, and also why my darn shoelace just won't stay down: the gravity is different.

And then I see the undead monster inside the cage. It's like a monstrous starfish—a five-armed beast, with a ferocious mouth at the center.

I grab the bone-shift to try to steer Seabiscuit away, but it's too late. Throngs of gorblins are scurrying toward us, buzzing with bloodthirsty anticipation. A dozen hop onto the taxi.

I lunge for the door just as it's yanked open. Gorblins swing in, jabbing their pronged tails. One gets me in the side, sending a sharp pain shooting through me.

"WE DON'T WANT WHAT YOU'RE SELLING!" Globlet shouts, as more of the vicious little creatures flood through the sunroof.

183

Another jab gets me in the back. I double over, tumbling out of the taxi. I feel a dozen tiny claws on me, some pushing, some pulling.

One jab gets me in the neck, and my head droops. They're pawing at my shoulders, pulling and dragging me. When I manage to lift my head, I realize they've hauled me to the battleball cage. The single door swings open, and three jabs in the back send me staggering, and I've got no choice but to go inside . . .

chapter sixteen

The fight hasn't even started yet, and Stargrove just knocked my fillings loose. A pack of gorblins wrangle the undead monster, dragging her to the cage's far wall.

Outside, Flustrod and Pillksort wave their little staffs around, addressing the crowd with the enthusiasm of someone selling a waffle iron on late-night TV. "We have two fighters! Stargrove: the only undefeated champion in the history of our beloved—and, admittedly, very cruel—game!"

The throng of gorblins erupts. They smack their tails together, a sort of high-five/clapping combo that creates an earsplitting rattle. One spins a Stargrove T-shirt over his head. Chants of "STARGROVE! STARGROVE!" fill the air.

I ignore the monsters, instead searching for Quint. As I look around, I realize even the bars of this cage are constructed from scavenged junk—different metals crisscrossing.

I let the strangely low gravity lift me higher, so I can get a better look, hoping to find Quint. But the crowd is too thick, with gorblins sitting on shoulders, stacked four and five high. No sign of my friends.

"And we also have . . ." Pillksort starts, then leans against the cage and whispers, "Hey, big top-dog liar, what's your name?"

"Um . . ." I hesitate, thinking it might not be smart to give my real name. They could realize

we're wanted by the enforcers—or worse, they
could be buddies with Wracksaw.

Also, a name that strikes fear in these
gorblins could be useful. But I'm coming up
with zero fear-striking names. Hard to put your
mind to cool names when a frothing zombified
starfish-beast is trying to break free and make
you its next meal.

"YOUR NAME!" Pillksort repeats.

With that, the gorblins slam the door shut, locking me inside with Stargrove. Just the two of us. And not for a candlelit dinner.

"STARGROVE VERSUS NEIL ARMSTRONG!" Flustrod shouts. I glimpse a dozen gorblins grabbing the cage, then—

"GIVE IT A SPIN . . ." Pillksort starts.

"Please don't give it a spin . . ." I murmur, but the gorblins are readying themselves.

"AND LET THE FIGHT BEGIN!"

With that, the cage is whirled like a top, and everything is a blur . . .

I'm flung around, completely helpless, no control over my body. I get a quick glimpse of Stargrove's upper arm, a split second before I smack into it and flip over it. I throw my arms out, but that does little to soften the impact as I careen into the wall. It feels like getting punched in the nose with a Buick.

It's quickly clear why Stargrove is undefeated: while I'm flipping and floating like . . . well . . . Neil Armstrong, her many arms keep her steadily buoyed.

The audience is hollering and whooping. Seems like it's been a long while since they've enjoyed one of their beloved fights . . .

I'm trying to figure out how to avoid another collision when the cage spins again. One of Stargrove's arms lashes out, clotheslining me with a fat whack to the throat. I'm gagging, doing a full midair somersault—

I slam into the cage wall again—and find myself face-to-face with Quint. Globlet, perched on his shoulder, tosses popcorn into her mouth.

"YOU GUYS ARE OK!" I exclaim.

"You're not," Globlet says, then pauses to chew. "You look like someone in trouble."

"YES, I KNOW THAT!" I shout as I wrap my fingers around the bars of the cage. "Quint, I need one of your big bright ideas. Like, *now*. This is like fighting a monster in the Gravitrooooonnn—"

My last word turns into a scream as Stargrove plucks me from the wall, yanking me off like I'm an old Band-Aid, then hurls me across the cage. I bounce off the metal bars, and before the pain even registers, I'm rebounding back. Stargrove's arms reach out, about to pull me into a brutal bear hug. Her wide mouth is open, and saliva drips from her fangs—falling *upward*. Three of the monster's arms are stretched wide, clinging above, below, and to the side.

"JACK!" I hear Quint yell, just as the cage spins and my world flips again—thankfully carrying me away from Stargrove.

Quint's face flashes past, a blur. I hear him cry out—

"Jack! You controlled Alfred without the Slicer, remember? Do the same thing now!"

"ALFRED WAS A ZOMBIE!" I cry.

"STARGROVE IS ALSO A ZOMBIE!"

Oh right. Zombie monster, monster zombie . . . still *undead*.

"BUT THAT CAUSED A LOT OF BAD STUFF TO HAPP—!" I don't finish that sentence, because I crash into Stargrove's back. It's sticky, like old jelly someone didn't clean up. I kick off.

"You're not in a position to turn down free advice!" Globlet cries, and I groan, 'cause she's right. My current position—knees against my chin, arms flailing—could be best described as "folded laundry."

The sphere is whipped into another rotation. But this time, I hold tight to the bars, using the Cosmic Hand's suckers to keep from being flung. I crawl up the side and quickly spin around, facing out, like a very bad impression of Spider-Man.

Back in the fortress, Ghazt did *something* to me. The hand changed. Its power changed. I just don't know *how to use it* . . .

But I need to figure it out. *Now.*

Stargrove is slowly pulling her way toward me. Her undead eyes flash with hunger. Hunger and something like confidence. She thinks she has me cornered.

Here goes . . . something? I think, as I extend the Cosmic Hand. I let the power wash over me, surge through my veins. I concentrate, reaching out with my thoughts like I did with Alfred at the water park, directing him to attack Blargus.

SKITCH!

That worked . . .

But will this?

Whatever Ghazt did to me . . . was it enough?

I keep my gaze focused on Stargrove,
staring into her eyes, trying to create some

sort of connection. Or, if there's some sort of connection that naturally exists between the Cosmic Hand and the undead, trying to tune the dial to find it.

There's a ringing in my ears—and I don't think it's just because of the multiple blows to the head I've endured over the past few minutes. Something's happening. And it's different from when I controlled Alfred.

The hand feels strange on my skin, like it's growing, morphing, strengthening. It's ice-cold. But I don't dare take my gaze away from Stargrove to look down at it.

At the water park, I couldn't sense what Alfred was thinking—I just hoped beyond hope my message would reach him.

This time, I know the message connects.

Stargrove pauses.

And her thoughts . . . I can *see* them.

I can't quite put it into words. What's in her mind is more like . . . an emoji. Man, I hate emoji, and I hope that if the world returns to something like normal, no one has any interest in emoji anymore.

I squeeze the Cosmic Hand, and the image from Stargrove's mind flashes and changes. I'm not going to call it an emoji. It's like a . . . mind-doodle.

Suddenly, I see *hundreds* of doodles. *Thousands!* Like a spinning kaleidoscope of emotions and actions.

But there are two that stand out, like they're highlighted and in bold. One is *anger*. The other is *gorblin*.

The doodles float in the air, visible only to me—like I'm wearing VR glasses that display the inner workings of Stargrove's psyche. And they're telling me Stargrove's had it with the gorblins.

Letting my thoughts go as simple as possible, I try to formulate a response.

Stargrove's expression changes as I conjure an image of the two of us, working together . . .

Flustrod can tell something's up, because he shouts, "SPIN! SPIN NOW!"

The cage whirls, but it doesn't matter. I grip one wall, Stargrove grips the other—and our eyes stay locked.

I throw out another mind-doodle: gorblins smashed like a game of Whac-A-Mole.

Let's do it!

The next second, Stargrove is hurling herself toward me. I launch off the wall, the low gravity allowing me to hang in the air. The cage spins around us. I reach out with my left hand, grabbing hold of Stargrove's mushy shoulder area, pulling myself toward her.

And then I see it.

The Cosmic Hand has *become* the Slicer—a hard, thick version of the blade, constructed from the hand's strange, fleshy substance.

No time to react to this newest horror, because—
"SPIN! SPIN! SPIN!"

Still gripping Stargrove, I gaze out, spotting
Quint. His shocked face breaks into a smile.

I direct Stargrove to open the cage—and with
one whack of her arm, it explodes in a burst of
tangled metal.

Flustrod staggers back, his face now awash in
fear. "RUN!"

"OUR BELOVED GAME IS NO LONGER FUN!"
Pillksort adds, turning to flee.

"You're gosh darn right it's not," I say softly, and
summon another thought: Stargrove, get 'em.

At once, her thick arms lash out, through the
door, grabbing gorblins by the dozen—

Apparently, my mind-doodle was enough to get Stargrove started, and her undead brain is now taking over. Her arms snap out, yanking gorblins into the cage.

"It's getting a little stuffy in here," I say to Stargrove, visualizing the words as I speak them. "How about we head out?"

Stargrove understands. She tosses the gorblins behind her and pulls herself toward the exit. Her mushy body flexes as she squeezes through the cage door, pulling me with her.

Outside, she flings her arms out again, and it's like watching a sheepdog wrangle an unwilling herd into their pen—but with a lot more flinging and flailing. Stargrove shoves the gorblins into the metal sphere any which way she can. Some get stuck between the grates; others are jammed together in a pile as the globe spins. They crawl and squirm over each other like a nest of bees.

Minutes later, Stargrove and I stand triumphant outside the cage, alongside Quint and Globlet. Seabiscuit sits nearby, bobbing playfully in the odd gravity.

"You know what you are?" Quint adds. "Bullies! Forcing creatures to fight. It's not a nice thing to do!"

"Even if it is entertaining!" Globlet says. I frown and give her a little poke.

Stargrove's emoji wheel spins, finally landing on an image that, for a moment, confuses me. Then I realize. It's *happiness*.

"Globlet!" I call as I head for Seabiscuit. "Let's go!"

She's busy making faces at the gorblins in the cage.

And then I realize my mistake.

Flustrod says, "Globlet, is it? Did he call you Globlet? As in, Globlet the Midnight Texter? Globlet the MOST WANTED?!"

Pillksort suddenly starts giggling. "And that means . . . *you* two must be the interdimensional interlopers."

"I'm telling everyone," Flustrod singsongs. He yanks out what appears to be a giant other-dimensional cell phone and starts tapping buttons.

I gulp.

"Jack," Quint calls. "This is one moment where I *will* suggest we are probably best off moving with haste."

In a flash, we're speeding away—toward the now-unguarded Weird River Crossing . . .

chapter
seventeen

We race for the crossing. I'm relieved to be leaving the gorblins behind—but know it's just a matter of time before Wracksaw and the enforcers close in, now that Flustrod has alerted everyone to our location.

I expect the crossing to be a bridge or walkway. Instead, it's a series of rocks, floating high above an antigravity river below. Seabiscuit navigates it with ease, bouncing and hopping forward. Through the window I spot Stargrove keeping pace. She still looks like a terrifying monster who could finish us all off with a flick of just one of her arms. But I'm not scared of her anymore. Especially not now, as she gleefully pinwheels over the rocks.

"So, are you gonna tell us the big dead star thing is our friend now?" Globlet asks, glancing suspiciously out the window at Stargrove. "'Cause we have a saying in my dimension: one is the loneliest number, two's company, three's more company, four is good for splitting pizza, and five is a bad idea all around, especially when the fifth is personally responsible for dozens of cage-match deaths."

I've finally calmed down enough to process and explain what's going on.

"What just happened . . ." I begin. "It was *different* than any other time I've controlled a zombie. With Alfred and the rest of my Zombie Squad, I just flick the Slicer while shouting out a command, like, 'Bring me nachos.' And they follow that command—which is why you so rarely see me without nachos. And when Blargus was gonna smash me . . . I controlled Alfred with *only* the Cosmic Hand, no Slicer. But I've never known what any of them were *thinking.*"

"Right," Quint says, leaning forward, tapping his fingers with extreme interest. "Continue . . ."

"But with Stargrove . . ." I start, explaining how I *saw* what Stargrove was thinking—the mind-doodles, a visible array of choices and options, allowing us to communicate. Not just me giving orders—but both of us, back and forth.

"Friend, that is extraordinary!" Quint exclaims. "You used a pictorial language to communicate with a monster zombie . . . and CONVINCED IT to help you in a fight that should have left you flattened!"

I nod, again thinking back to my final moments with Ghazt.

The final few molecules of Ghazt's power were delivered into the Cosmic Hand. I saw it change, I freaked, and Ghazt simply said, "Now you are the general, Jack."

I didn't know what he meant then. But I think now I do. To lead an army, you need to be able to communicate with its solders. And that power of communication seems to be what Ghazt put into the Cosmic Hand.

"If I can read the zombies' mind-doodles, and they can understand mine," I say, a smile growing on my face, "that could be how I lead the army."

"Are you settled on calling them 'mind-doodles'?" Globlet asks. "'Cause I have notes."

Ignoring Globlet, Quint says, "If you can actually do that . . ." He doesn't need to finish his sentence. We both know it could turn the tide in the coming battle for the future of our dimension.

"I won't know for sure until I've got a *lot* of zombies to try with," I caution. "Maybe it just works with Stargrove because we have, like, a special psychic connection."

"Hang on to your biscuits!" Globlet shouts, as Seabiscuit bounds off the last floating rock, flips in the strange gravity, and finally lands on the far side of the crossing.

What lies before us now is a very wide, very exposed road. "Are there any other routes to the Hidden City?" I ask. "It's too easy for Wracksaw and the enforcers to find us on these main roads. Thanks to those gorblins, the whole dimension knows where to look for us."

"Ah, so you want options? Well, you're in luck! We have options! Two!" Globlet says, pointing to a sign ahead.

THE FUN AND EASY ROUTE
INCLUDES FREE CAR WASH

THE HIGHWAY OF HAZARDS
‖ߖ℞∴ⵜⵝⵯ ⴽⵑ↓⊁

TAKE A RIDE AND SEE DOUBLE DANGEROUS DETOURS!
RADIOACTIVE ROADBLOCKS!
COUNTLESS BOOBY TRAPS!
PERIL APLENTY!
DEFINITELY QUICKSAND!

"Peril aplenty." It sounds like a decent theme for a birthday party . . . and a terrible theme for the final stretch to the Hidden City. But if it keeps us off Wracksaw's radar, I'll take it . . .

Turns out, it's way more than just peril. The route is both impossible and impassible.

Or, it *would be*, if we didn't have Stargrove. Now that we're trading mind-doodles, she's Swiss Army knife–level helpful.

"We're getting so close," Globlet says, tapping the windshield. "Next stop, Hidden City!"

Just then, the GPS chimes. It's the same alert sound I've heard about two hundred times now. It means there's some can't-miss attraction nearby.

Globlet leans forward. "Ooh, we're not too far from *my very favorite monument*!"

"You have a favorite monument?" I ask.

"Doesn't everyone?" Quint says.

"It's this big statue called Champions' Last Hurrah," Globlet tells us. "It's a super-famous marker at the site of the final big battle between the Champions and one of Ṛeżżőch's evil servants. At the time, everyone thought it was the *last* of Ṛeżżőch's servants, so they put up this monument and a little museum and souvenir stand. And a *crazy good* Froyo shop."

"Ṛeżżőch's *last* servant?" I ask. "But—"

Globlet sighs. "Yep, they were wrong. There was some other servant nobody knew about who wound up waking up big Ṛeżży. So . . ."

In the rearview mirror, I see Quint's staring at me, eyebrows raised, curious. And not curious like he wants to know what flavors of Froyo they have. Curious, like . . . this could be important.

I don't want to change direction right now. We're so close to the Hidden City. Except . . . a bunch of monster warriors thought they'd destroyed *all* Rężżőch's servants. But they actually failed. And it might help us to know why, before we try to destroy Rężżőch himself.

"Let's go," I say. It's just a small detour. And what we learn could be too valuable to pass up.

I jerk the wheel, steering Seabiscuit through the wild, overgrown rock jungle that separates our perilous path from the main road. Stargrove follows, loping behind us as Seabiscuit weaves and bounds her way toward the GPS signal.

Nearing the main road, I ease Seabiscuit into a crawl. I glance both ways down the long roadway. No one coming, no one going. I take a deep breath and turn onto the main path. Toward Champions' Last Hurrah.

"Now! If you look out the window to your right, you might just catch a glimpse of . . ." Globlet announces, jumping into her perky tour-guide routine. But she quickly turns solemn. "You'll catch a glimpse of never-ending despair. Don't worry if you miss it, you'll have plenty more opportunities to glimpse never-ending despair. That's what most of my dimension is now. Never-ending despair."

We travel through a series of abandoned towns and outposts, each one in worse shape than the last. Glowing eyes peer out from piles of rubble, then quickly retreat into the shadows as we pass. Sagging buildings wail sadly. I suspect they're alive in the way a cactus is alive. Sits there, doesn't do a whole lot, but you're still sort of a jerk if you kick it for no reason.

It's like a hurricane ripped through this place, and no one rebuilt it. From the vacant stare in Globlet's eyes, I know: that hurricane was Ṛeżżőch.

In the distance, I see a cluster of buildings—and something huge rising up, towering over them. "That's it. Champions' Last Hurrah," Globlet says, sitting up in her seat. "Me and my gal pals used to stop here for smoothies and hijinks. But . . . it used to be a whole bunch more crowded."

"Hey, Globlet," I say. "Is that a—"

"Skeleton? Why yes, it is, Jack. Quite an astute observation," she says, with a massive eye roll. Then she quickly murmurs, "Sorry . . . I'm bummed out now. Yeah, it's a skeleton. That's part of the monument."

"And it's not just a skeleton. There are two figures there," Quint says as Seabiscuit slows to a stop.

Soon, Quint and I are standing on the rough road, in the shadow of the monument.

The first figure is a skeleton. I've seen a lot of skeletons—*fought* a lot of skeletons. But this one is different. It takes me a moment to realize why—and then Quint voices what I'm thinking. "Jack, this is the same species of monster as Blarg . . . except much, much bigger."

Blarg was the first of the servants of Ŗeżżŏċħ that I slew.

But it's what we see next that really melts my brain. The second figure. The monument shows this Blarg-like creature is locked in battle with . . . Thrull.

chapter eighteen

"Quint . . ." I say, trembling.

"I see it," he says.

"Why is Thrull doing battle with a servant of Ṛeżżŏcħ when he himself *is* a servant of Ṛeżżŏcħ?" I ask. "And why is there a *monument* to Thrull?"

"Also, why did they make Thrull so tall?!" Quint adds. "The scale is nonsensical."

"Dramatic license!" a perky voice says.

I spin around, startled. A monster stands outside what must be the visitors' center, looking very eager to chat. Beside her is a booth selling Thrull action figures, little baggies claiming to contain "authentic Thrull chest-hair fibers," and about two thousand magnets. "You folks must be interested in a guided tour!"

We have zero time for a tour, guided or otherwise. "No, actually. We're in a rush," I say. "Just wanted to know what happened—"

"Please save all questions for the end of the tour," she says curtly.

"But—"

Quint grins. "Not a problem!"

I sigh. There's nothing Quint loves more than a guided tour. His dream is probably a guided tour of a tour-guide school.

"Wonderful!" the monster says, scuttling out from behind the booth. She's got, at minimum, eight pairs of legs and three wide, bulging eyes. Her voice is high-pitched and she talks so fast, all the words overlap. "My name is Amarelda, and I'll be your guide!"

"Do you get, um . . . a lot of visitors here?" I ask.

"SURE DO!" she says, then stops to think. "Correction: sure DID! After Ŗeżżőcħ and the portals and that bad stuff . . . visitation has dipped."

Amarelda suddenly shoves out a small, toad-like monster, holding it by a flabby fold of neck skin. "Donations are encouraged," Amarelda says, and the toad-monster's mouth slowly opens.

"OK," I say.

"*Strongly* encouraged," Amarelda adds.

We nod and smile.

Amarelda turns to Stargrove, and I shoot her a quick mind-doodle: save your money.

Finally, Amarelda tucks the frog back into a pouch and launches into her routine. "The skeleton is Horgaz, once believed to be the last of Ŗeżżőcħ's great servants. In the very spot where you now stand, on the street now known as Warrior's Way, Horgaz was slain by the Great Champions."

THE FINISHING BLOW WAS DELIVERED BY THRULL, THE MOST LEGENDARY OF THE GREAT CHAMPIONS! AND NOW, HIS TRIUMPHANT MOMENT IS PRESERVED IN TIME FOREVER!

POW!

"There were Great Champions?" I ask. "And Thrull was . . . one of them?"

"Of course!" Amarelda says. "Oh, help me, is *Most Important Events in the History of Forever* no longer part of a young monster's curriculum? The Great Champions were an unstoppable team, tracking and battling the servants of Ŗeżżőch. They were the most bonded of companions and the most accomplished of warriors. And this was their finest moment! A victory for the ages!"

"It was?" I stare.

"Absolutely. At the time it was believed that Horgaz was the very last of Ṛeżżőcħ's great servants. Ṛeżżőcħ slept—and so when Thrull slew Horgaz, the entire world believed no creature remained who would awaken Ṛeżżőcħ again. It was the Champions' last hurrah. Which is why this monument is called . . . Champions' Last Hurrah!"

Amarelda keeps talking, but I don't hear what she says. I'm trying to put these pieces together, but nothing fits. When I entered the monster dimension, did I also enter some kind of alternate universe where Thrull is . . . a good guy?? I feel like I'm hallucinating.

My mind's racing, processing this new information. The very first of Ṛeżżőcħ's servants that I killed was a Blarg-creature—and that triggered so much of what followed. Slaying Blarg is what set me on this path, what led to where I am today.

And now Amarelda is saying that the *last* of Ṛeżżőcħ's evil servants ever to be killed was *also* a Blarg-creature. Slain by Thrull.

I take a shaky step toward the statue of Thrull, staring up. He's lean and wiry. His beard is well-groomed.

Amarelda says, "That is precisely how Thrull appeared when he felled Horgaz! And he only grew more handsome, I hear. Wink wink."

You mean more monstrous, I think.

I don't like this. It's not helping anything. It makes me uneasy to learn that Thrull fought the same type of creature that I did. I don't want to have anything in common with Thrull.

"It's very peculiar," Quint agrees. "What's next—are we going to see Thrull's tree house fortress where he hung out with his buddies?"

I shoot Quint a hard glare. The first time I've ever looked at my best buddy like that. I quickly lower my head. "We never should have stopped here," I say softly.

"So . . . what went wrong?" Quint asks Amarelda. "You said the Champions thought no one would awaken Ŗeżżőch again . . . but someone clearly did."

"Great question!" Amarelda says. "With Horgaz felled, the Great Champions thought their work was done. We all thought the world was safe. But Ŗeżżőch *did* awaken. And do you know how that happened?"

"No," Globlet says.

"Darn," Amarelda says. "Me neither."

"Sounds like a question for Shuggoth!" Quint says.

At the word *Shuggoth*, Amarelda suddenly twitches. Shudders. She looks us over. And then her eyes fix on the Cosmic Hand.

A tremor runs through her. Her many eyeballs dart around, then freeze.

One eyeball cracks, and black liquid seeps out . . .

Her head spins. Her body spasms. Her eyes quake in their sockets. A groan gurgles from her throat as she starts thrashing about, all of her twisting, twitching. Suddenly, she snaps rigid, and a voice—a different voice—erupts from some awful place deep inside her . . .

I recoil in horror, jumping back, nearly tripping over Quint. I hear Seabiscuit's fingers drum the ground nervously.

"We gotta shut her up!" I cry.

"Is this not part of the tour?" Globlet asks.

"No!"

"HEY, LADY!" Globlet shouts. "I *strongly encourage* you to chill out!"

And then—Amarelda falls. She lies on the ground, mumbling softly. Gibberish. She begins pawing at the ground, digging, then—at last—using her many legs to disappear into the sand . . .

chapter nineteen

I'm bent over, hands on my knees, trying to stop my heart from exploding. Unfortunately, the horror doesn't stop.

"What is it, Seabiscuit?" Globlet calls.

I turn. Seabiscuit has lifted one finger and is pointing down the road. I see a cloud of dust on the horizon, then—

Wracksaw has found us.

I can't believe it.

"No, no," I stammer out. "No! We're *so close!* We have come too far to just get killed in a stupid, cheap, other-dimensional tourist trap!"

We're overpowered and outnumbered. Quint's conjurer's cannon is busted, and the Louisville Slicer is back in the human dimension—we don't even have weapons.

I glance away from Wracksaw, down the main road toward the Hidden City. The direction we were going—until we decided to stop here, because of . . .

Thrull.

I can almost feel the statue looming over me. Taunting me.

"I estimate four minutes," Quint says. "Until the enemy is here."

I turn, scanning the site for . . . what? A last-minute jumbo cannon, hidden away? An army of carapaces coming to our rescue? 101 Wracksaw-hating dalmatians?

There's nothing.

What would June and Dirk do?

What would Rover do?

EEK!

BASH!

"Guys, why the long faces?" Globlet says. "I mean, Jack, you just happen to have a very long face . . . But come on, we can do this!"

I can't believe that *Globlet* is now the one rallying *us*.

She plops onto the ground, which is made of what looks like black sand. Globlet uses a finger to start tracing out a plan, and each new line reveals some new color. When she's finished, the ground is a series of green, orange, yellow, pink, and turquoise zigzags. I'm trying to follow what Globlet is suggesting, but it's sort of a blur and I don't really think that's my fault.

"Classic pincer maneuver to begin. Jack, you spin around eleven times, then double back for the statue. That's the key, obviously—and that's also the trap. Because while you're on spin number nine, Seabiscuit begins jogging in place. Quint, your bowling shoes will be essential. Dumb question, but I have to ask—"

I look to Quint and, for maybe the first time ever, I see that he does *not* immediately comprehend something.

Seabiscuit seems to get it, though, index finger bobbing up and down slowly, like she's in agreement with every detail of Globlet's plan. Stargrove just sways back and forth.

"So . . ." Globlet says, clapping her hands, a cloud of colors puffing out. Seabiscuit sneezes. "What do you think?"

Wracksaw enters Warrior's Way atop his horribly altered strayfur. It's as big as a horse, with ill-fitting, misshapen legs. I do a double take when I realize that one leg appears to be on backward. It causes me to shiver, and to think back to the carcass pile in Wracksaw's fortress's laboratory.

I gulp.

He looks very much in command, relaxed and comfortable. But as his strayfur slows to a stop, I notice two of Wracksaw's armacles intertwined, fidgeting—and I get the sense that he's trying *really hard* to look like a boss monster—albeit one that's mutated, half-melted, and disfigured.

I remember Thrull treating Wracksaw like nothing but a minion, coolly striding away once he'd gotten what he'd wanted. And I remember the tantrum that followed. Must have really done a number to Wracksaw's already fragile ego.

High in the air, trailing behind him like a storm cloud, are hundreds, maybe thousands of strayfurs. They move at short, sharp angles, staying aloft, ready to attack at any moment.

Beside him, Eye-Bulb suddenly perks up. "I see it! The hand vehicle camouflaged with racing stripes! I found it, sir! And now, to find the boy . . ."

"He's right here!" Wracksaw says. "They're all right here!"

"OK, good, sir. I just wanted to make sure you knew."

Here we are, in the middle of Warrior's Way, looking absolutely nothing like warriors. We look more like four idiots who just got busted playing a game of marbles.

There's only one thing left to do, and that's beg. I get to one knee, resting my hand like I'm a quarterback about to detail the big play to win the game.

Wracksaw, do we have to just keep doing this? I mean, c'mon.

Do you ever just sit down with a good book? Or plop down on the couch and watch a movie with friends? What if we tried that?

Maybe we'd realize that we have way more in common than we think.

"He does enjoy moving images!" Debra calls. "He watches recordings of his own surgeries. Repeatedly. Again and again and again. Then he has us watch them. And if we doze off, we get the zap-tap."

Wracksaw chuckles. "It's true. We watched the surgeries I performed on myself . . . after what *you* did to me," he says, staring daggers at me.

I frown. "You're welcome?"

"I told you, Jack, that I was upgraded. That the pain you caused me gave me the opportunity to modify myself for the better. Would you like to see?" Wracksaw asks, sounding like some kid you get stuck on a playdate with who has, like, *every toy* and is very excited to show them to you one by one.

"I would *totally* like to see!" Globlet says, waving her hand around.

Wracksaw rocks back on his tentacle-legs, then stabs two sharp armacle tips into his chest, prying open a long, not quite healed stitch. He pulls it apart, splitting his torso right down the middle. "Witness terror!" he says, his torso yawning wider until out comes . . .

Wracksaw snatches up the remote and flings it at Eye-Bulb. "Now you have it back. Speak to me like that again, and I will merge you with a *third* creature. And this one you will *not* like."

"Worse than Debra?" Eye-Bulb asks.

"That's not nice," Debra says. "I like you. We get to talk so much more now."

Wracksaw ignores them, quickly jamming his chest back together, muttering. "*Enough* of this nonsensical, pre-death banter. You destroyed my fortress. You aided Ghazt in creating a vortex that caused me more pain than I knew was possible. Now I will enjoy *your* pain . . ."

With that, Wracksaw whips one of his armacles upward, then brings it slicing down, rigid, pointing directly at us. "Strayfurs, attack!"

Instantly, everything is a blur.

The strayfurs come swooping down from all sides. Beaks snapping, talons slashing. One's mouth opens wide, and I see a thousand tiny fangs spiraling down its throat.

Wracksaw begins to cackle. "Not too quickly!" he calls. "The boy must suffer as I did."

The strayfurs swarm toward us, hungry, ferocious.

"Behind the statue!" Quint shouts, running back down the street. Globlet and Seabiscuit join him, and all three of them slide into cover.

I zip a follow me! mind-doodle to Stargrove, and she stomps after me.

But the strayfurs come after me, too.

As we near the statue, I clamber up onto Stargrove's back, like a kid at a parade getting a better view. I shoot her a mind-doodle: tear these foul strayfurs apart, please.

Stargrove's own mind-doodle forms in response—

"No!" I cry. "Not me, *them*!"

Our mind-doodles worked so well before, but now that my life is on the line, it's all falling apart.

But then, Stargrove sends another mind-doodle—this one of her laughing.

"You were joking?" I ask. "OK, *now* you decide to have sense of humor?!"

Then Stargrove lashes out with three of her arms. I'm tossed backward, into the crook between two of her arms, holding on like an oversized backpack. And Stargrove, who has never lost a fight, begins to attack.

Her arms are a rapid-fire flurry, plucking strayfurs from the air, jamming them into her mouth, a single *chomp!*, and then tossing them aside. It's brutal and efficient

I zip her another mind-doodle: stay here in front of the statue, and don't let any strayfurs pass.

She doesn't even acknowledge me, just keeps grabbing strayfurs with every one of her arms. I jump off her back, then scramble around the base of the statue, diving and rolling before collapsing next to Quint and Globlet.

Catching my breath, I look to Quint. I'm hoping there's some brilliant idea knocking around in that brain of his. Stargrove can hold off our assailants for a while. But not forever.

Quint's staring off into the distance, lost in thought. And then, suddenly, his eyes light up.

Yes! I'm certain we're saved. My genius friend has figured out some way out of this mess, some way to keep us—

"A key chain!" he says, grabbing it off the ground and stuffing it into his pocket.

My jaw just about hits the floor.

"I was hoping I'd find one of these," he says.

I glare at him, feeling like I've lost all understanding of *everything*. He looks back at me with relief, like he really, truly needed that key chain.

Meanwhile, Globlet is once again pulling my camera from her belly. And I don't like that, either. I mean, that camera is important to me! It's the thing that got me through the first few months of the apocalypse. It was my connection to June. Without it, I would never have spoken to her, at least not for more than just a few dumb, clumsy sentences.

I look back and forth between them. "WHAT IS WITH YOU TWO?" I finally exclaim.

"Whatcha mean?" Globlet asks.

I sigh. "OK, not you as much. All the things that I sort of already suspected about you were confirmed. Plus you're a criminal, which I hadn't expected but really just adds depth to your personality. But as for you, Quint . . ."

MORE SOUVENIRS?! Seriously? The strayfurs are upon us, Wracksaw is **right there**, and you want a **key chain** right now?!

I mean, I get it. You go to another dimension, you want to come home with something. But . . .

I put my head in my hands. "Look, I'm sure Neil Armstrong and Buzz—actually, not those two, they were pretty serious dudes, but the *other guy*—I bet the other guy probably wanted to bring home a souvenir. But—"

"They brought home moon rocks," Quint says flatly. "Tons of them."

"YOU KNOW WHAT I MEAN! Quint, you've been totally out to lunch the whole time we've been in this dimension. And yes, that's made this last hurrah of ours the best last hurrah anybody ever had. And I say that totally aware that we're sitting beneath a monument to last hurrahs. But please . . . WHAT IS GOING ON WITH YOU?"

From the other side of the monument, Wracksaw calls out, "Debra-Bulb, kill the star-shaped creature. I'm ready to end this."

"Hey, you guys," Globlet says, "I think you're probably about to die. Probably not me, because I'm super resourceful, but definitely you. So . . . Quint, you should tell him."

"Tell me what?" I ask. "Do I have something in my teeth? Have I had something in my teeth this whole time?"

"Quint, tell him," Globlet says.

"Globlet, stop," Quint says. "Jack, there's nothing I have to tell you. We just have to get out of here, find the Hidden City, and talk to Shuggoth because I believe that we *can* triumph in this dimension."

I definitely think he's hiding something, but before I can press the issue, I hear Wracksaw's voice.

YOU HAVE TOYED WITH THINGS THAT YOU DO NOT UNDERSTAND, JACK. YOU WIELD THE COSMIC HAND, BUT YOU KNOW NOT HOW OR WHY.

I glance back.

Strayfur carcasses are scattered across the street. From atop his mount, Wracksaw calls, "Not smart, Jack. Do you think I—genius, scientist, poker, prodder—use tools without knowing their purpose?"

"Now," Wracksaw says, "you will die here, so very far from home, farther from home than any of your species has ever died, I suspect. So that's kind of neat, right?"

At once, the remaining strayfurs dive again, descending like a black curtain, turning the sky dark.

Globlet gives Seabiscuit a whack on the leg, and together they sprint toward a long building in the distance. It has one door and long windows made of something resembling rock candy.

They've got the right idea, I think, watching Seabiscuit force her way through the door.

"Come on, Quint," I say, and take off running.

Strayfurs swoop left and right around the monument. Others go high, then dive-bomb, trying to get past Stargrove. But she's like a soccer goalie with all the cheat codes on. Arms lashing out, swinging up, swatting strayfurs, grabbing strayfurs, and, more often than not, jamming them into her mouth, tearing off chunks so that they can never be a threat again. She's biting into them like she's at a buffet with six minutes until closing, and she's gonna get her money's worth.

"I must say, as much as I disliked those gorblins," Quint says, running alongside me, "I'm quite happy we bumped into them."

We burst into the long building at the end of Warrior's Way. It trembles just slightly, reacting to our presence. At first, I think the wide, arched doorway has beads dangling in front of it—but as I push through, they feel more like long strands of string cheese.

With a quick glance around, I see we're in a museum dedicated to the battle that Amarelda described. Huge glowing images on the walls recreate climactic moments of combat. Weapons are displayed throughout the room, along with faint, almost holographic images of the different warriors who wielded them.

Globlet has just finished fiddling with the taxi's bumper as we enter; then she's hopping off, whistling to herself as she hurries toward one of the weapons: a thick chain, as long as a fire hose, each link as big as a Frisbee. Globlet—showing strength I never suspected she had—grabs it and pulls it toward Seabiscuit.

"Oh, Globlet . . . YES!" I say, watching her run around. "Your plan to get us out of here was real? I thought maybe you were just doing that thing you do where you're . . ."

"Kooky," Quint supplies.

Suddenly, there's a loud *WHACK* at one of the museum's windows. Then another. Strayfurs. Getting past Stargrove. I need to call her back—I can't just leave her out there like some living (unliving?) shield. She can't stop them all—and it's not right. I didn't free her from that horrible battleball just to be a strayfur sponge.

Quint asks, "Globlet, what can we do to help?"

"Not a thing!" she says cheerfully. "I made up this idea with my gal pals years ago. Just never had a taxi or any other vehicle to pull it off."

"Wait, what?" I ask. "What're you talking about?"

The plan to steal the monument and sell it to the Society of Stolen Monuments. They pay top dollar.

GLOBLET, WE'RE **NOT** TRYING TO STEAL A MONUMENT!

She shrugs. "Well, that's what *I'm* trying to do."

"And you think that's what *we're* trying to do?" I ask.

"Well, I just assumed," she says. "You see a big monument, you want to take it, right?"

I manage to speak through gritted teeth. "No, Globlet, we are trying to escape! Not with statues . . . with *our lives!*"

"Oh," Globlet says, "I guess I see why that would be of more interest to you than a very large monument to the creature who murdered Bardle, your best monster friend."

I throw my hands up and turn around, pacing.

"I apologize, Jack!" she says. "I cannot be forgiven. I failed. And now I will have your deaths upon my conscience the rest of my days."

"Also your death, Globlet," Quint notes, as three more strayfurs slam into the window, bits of the strange glass splintering.

I carefully peer outside. Stargrove continues to dismantle the evil bird creatures, chomping into them at incredible speed. The street around her is littered with their lifeless bodies. She'd absolutely *crush it* at a hot-dog-eating contest. But . . . there are too many. She can't be everywhere at once.

Suddenly, a strayfur bursts through the door!
It zips around, slamming into a dozen weapons,
a metallic clattering sound ringing out. The
strayfur ricochets off a heavy shield, arcing,
spiraling, then speeding toward Seabiscuit.
Seabiscuit simply raises one finger, then—

It's time to face facts:
Globlet's escape plan is not an escape plan at all.
The strayfurs are getting past Stargrove.
No one's coming to our rescue.
If we're going down—which we are—I'm gonna
go down fighting.

chapter twenty

I march toward one of the weapons the strayfur
knocked over. It's an enormous blade made
from some metal we don't have on Earth. It
must weigh a hundred pounds. But, thanks to
the Cosmic Hand, I'm able to lift and wield it,
though just barely.

"Quint," I say, "I'm gonna go punch Wracksaw
in the nose. Wanna come?"

"Indeed, friend," he says.

"And if we live through that," I say, "then
you're gonna tell me the thing you're not telling
me."

Quint tilts his head. He's thinking, about to
speak, when—

The ceiling splits above us! It's ripped off like
the top of a tin can. Light pours in, so that—for
a moment—the figure above us is only a huge,
looming shadow.

Wracksaw dismounts his strayfur, clumsily sliding over the top of the monster, mashing its head into the jagged ledge where the ceiling was torn off. I hear a muted howl from the strayfur— then spot its body, mangled and broken, heaving over the ledge as Wracksaw descends.

I spin around, looking for Stargrove. Instead I

hear stampeding feet and then feel a sharp pain as Debra-Bulb bursts through the door, nicking my side with one of their long blades.

Wracksaw moves forward, howling with maniacal laughter as one armacle smacks me. Light flares behind my eyes. Sharp, exploding pain sends a scream up my throat—but it's silenced as Wracksaw's next blow knocks me out of the museum, the window shattering, rock-candy glass flying, black sand kicking up as I hit the street and tumble end over end.

I manage to lift my head, which feels like a fifty-pound bowling ball. Black sand on my lips. My whole body feels like a stubbed toe—hot, sharp, stinging pain. Rolling over, I realize I managed to hang on to the huge blade. The Cosmic Hand's nearly magnetic suction-cup grip kept it in my hand.

A cloud of sand billows past. Squinting, eyes burning, I see Wracksaw speeding toward me on tentacle legs—his movement is something between a slide, a glide, and a slither.

One armacle snaps back, the air cracking then whistling as it comes crashing down.

I can barely lift my weapon chest-high—but it's just enough, and it's just in time. The armacle crashes against the blade, violently twisting my wrist, slamming my shoulder into the ground. Without the Cosmic Hand, the weapon would be halfway to Pluto right now, sent flying like a paper football flicked by Donkey Kong.

Wracksaw circles, gifting me a split second to breathe. My eyes dart, blinking away stinging tears, scanning the museum, then—

Stargrove! I see her, and I shoot her a quick mind-doodle: Stargrove, attacking Wracksaw.

Her response is near-instant. The ground quakes as she rumbles down Warrior's Way, looking like a wrestler racing down the ramp, about to dive into the ring and join the fight. A dozen long, heavy strides—and then she's there, launching herself into the air, limbs outstretched, looking like a two-ton throwing star in a belly-flop contest.

But then, with startling speed, Wracksaw spins, armacle raising. I hear a syrupy explosion sound, and about a billion little beads burst out of Wracksaw's armacle. A buzz fills the air.

I know that sound, but this is tinier, weaker— like a familiar song played through cheap portable speakers.

Strayfurs, I realize. But the size of plump houseflies. Like . . . strayfur larvae.

Most slam into Stargrove. Others zip past her, exploding against the wall of the visitors' center like a swarm of thumbnail-sized water balloons.

The eruption looks like a crate of silly string was detonated. Stargrove hits the wall. I expect her to rebound immediately . . . but she doesn't. She seems to be stuck, the larva goo holding her in place like superglue. Her many arms struggle, but she can't free herself.

Stargrove flashes two mind-doodles: Stuck. Gross.

My heart sinks. Stargrove, the undefeated fighter, is down for the count. She got us this far, but she can't take us any farther. But then I hear—

"Swing one of your arm tentacles at Jack again," Quint says, "and I will summon a conjuration so powerful it will turn you inside out."

I spin. Quint is wielding his conjurer's cannon! But it looks different . . .

Wracksaw chuckles. "I am the one creature who feels no fear from that threat. As I was carried through that awful portal you children opened, I *was* turned inside out. And then outside in. And then inside out, outside in, inside out, outside in, again, again, again. I kept track: nine hundred seventy-five times."

I pinch my hoodie. "This hoodie is reversible. You can wear it inside out or outside in and it doesn't matter. So, it wouldn't care either."

Ha. Check and mate.

"Hoodies are not creatures, fool!" Wracksaw spits. "I said the *one creature*—not the *one creature and/or article of clothing*."

Darn it, he's right.

Wracksaw swivels toward Quint. "And do not attempt to threaten me with a different conjuration—any would be equally worthless. You were spotted by many during your journey, and all reported the same thing: Your weapon was destroyed before you came to this dimension. You are powerless."

I see the device in Quint's hand, and I suddenly understand why he needed to stop everywhere on our journey. I knew he was tinkering with it, but didn't realize he was *rebuilding it from souvenirs.* Everything he was gathering along the way had a purpose. Even the key chain, which moments earlier caused me to snap at him, is affixed to the side, holding two pieces of the cannon together.

"Yes, his cannon got busted up, but he rebuilt it into something better," I say proudly. "That's what Quint *does*!"

Although, I think, *that doesn't explain what he won't tell me.*

"Of course," I say, with zero hesitation.

Quint and Wracksaw stare each other down for what feels like an eternity. It seems like it might never end until, very slowly and awkwardly, Debra-Bulb comes veering onto the scene.

"Left!" Debra says.

"Right!" Eye-Bulb says.

"Left!" Debra says.

It's like watching a pair of toddlers try to run their first three-legged race.

"Good job, sir!" Debra says.

"Sir, the job you're doing is very good!" Eye-Bulb adds.

"I said it was good first, sir," points out Debra.

"I said it was *very* good," Eye-Bulb says.

Wracksaw turns to them and roars. "Enough! I am sick of listening to the two of you argue. Every single utterance goes right up my spine. Or would, if I had a spine." Wracksaw pauses. "To be clear, I'm not implying that I'm spineless, as in scared. Only that my physical form does not contain a spine."

"We knew what you meant, sir," Debra says.

"Always do! That's why you're the best!" Eye-Bulb adds. "Um, anyone seen my eye?"

The patterns across Wracksaw's flesh swirl in a full-body eye roll. His armacle quickly lifts and erupts, and a fresh swarm of strayfur pupae is launched, pinning Debra-Bulb to the wall, half-draped across Stargrove.

I expect Quint to go all Master Conjurer on Wracksaw right then. But he doesn't. He just stands there.

I swallow. Was Wracksaw right? *Is* Quint bluffing?

He returns my look and bites his lip. And then his arms drop to his side.

My heart sinks. We're sunk.

Wracksaw's face twists into a cruel grin. "What did you say a moment earlier, Jack? 'He rebuilt it into something better. That's what Quint *does*!' Apparently not!" Wracksaw chuckles. "But that is what *I* do. Did I mention the unknowable number of experimental augmentations and alterations I performed on myself? A near-ceaseless parade of procedures! Made possible only because of my body's reaction to being sent through the portal. Did I mention that?"

"Yeah," I say. "The whole inside-out, outside-in thing. We heard about it."

"It's not enough just to hear about it," Wracksaw says, two armacles sliding toward his stomach. "You must *see*!"

"Oh, the TV remote thing?" I ask. "Hey, Quint, you like magic, watch this. He's gonna barf a remote out of his belly."

Wracksaw ignores me. "You got a small glimpse," he says, as the patterns across his body swirl and slide. "But this is really going to wow you."

Wracksaw pads toward me. "Your five-pointed friend is now graffiti on the wall. Your conjurer has no powers. And I am done talking, regretfully for all of us."

Wracksaw's armacles snake through the slit in his stomach, prying it open, peeling back layer after layer of flesh, revealing a tangled, pulsing . . . something.

I jerk my head back, recoiling in disgust. Quint looks torn between losing his lunch and wanting a peek at whatever horror this is.

Inside Wracksaw's open stomach, I see a tangled ball of shiny *somethings,* wriggling around, climbing over each other. One slides out and drops to the ground. Then another. Then they begin to stir, like they're coming out of some hibernation. In a moment, they're flooding the ground. Awful things, half-slithering, half-scampering—like a ferret combined with a snake.

One circles around Wracksaw's leg tentacles, leaving dark, oily streaks on his skin.

Then, at once, they spring to attention—like they're suddenly aware they are no longer confined to Wracksaw's insides.

"Quint, let's go," I half-whisper.

But Wracksaw just laughs. "You," he says to Quint, quietly, "are no longer needed here."

At once, the vermin swarm toward Quint. He staggers back, falls, and tries to stand—but they're on him, skittering up his legs, dangling from his clothes. They don't bite or chew. They just envelop him. Working together, the creatures are like an anaconda, tightening around Quint.

"GET 'EM OFF!" Quint cries, wildly swiping at his head and torso.

"Quint, I'm coming!" I cry, but then an armacle crashes down, stopping me short. I move to leap over the armacle, but it pushes me back, knocks me down. And when I stand . . . I don't see Quint. He's buried beneath a mound of Wracksaw's writhing, wriggling rodents.

My hand tightens around the sword's handle. "GET THOSE THING OFF HIM! RIGHT NOW!" I shout. Fear and fury fill me as I tug the blade.

Wracksaw watches me try to lift it. "You really think your ridiculous hand is fit to wield that weapon?"

No, I think. *No, no, no.*

I raise my head slowly, looking up at the statue. I'm wielding the blade that belonged to Thrull. The one Thrull used, in this spot, to slay Horgaz. *That's* the weapon I chose from the museum.

I feel light-headed. Dizzy.

I grab the handle, fingers tight around it like it can keep me from falling.

"Hold on to that sword, Jack," Wracksaw says. "While the monster who held it previously . . . now ends your life."

There's a flash of foul monstrous flesh, blades erupting through Wracksaw's skin, as one razor-sharp armacle slices through the air. It strikes downward, splitting the monument in two. The two combatants fall away from each other.

It seems to happen in slow motion. The servant Horgaz falls to the side. And Thrull topples forward. Toward me. Darkness falls over me like a tidal wave.

I take a quick step back, starting to run. But my foot slips on a dead strayfur, and my leg goes out. I go down—crashing to the ground, scrambling back up, desperate to—

Too late. The statue is upon me. I can do nothing but throw one arm over my face and wait for my life to flash before my eyes.

An earsplitting crash shakes the ground.

But . . . I don't feel it.

I wait a second longer.

Life still hasn't flashed before my eyes.

OK, I know the first thirteen years weren't the greatest—but c'mon, it got interesting after that.

I finally open my eyes . . .

Very slowly, I peer around the statue. And I hear . . . Globlet?

"That's right!" she says. She's yelling at a very confused Wracksaw. "They don't call me Globlet the Monument Nabber 'cause I *don't* nab monuments. I had a whole plan to heist that thing, and you messed it up! But I'm still taking this half!"

I crane my neck.

Oh, hey, Jack! You think this'll fit in the trunk? I was thinking if we roll the windows down, kinda hook it, then—

I'm not sure what to do first. Kick Wracksaw?
Hug Globlet?

No! Check on Quint. But as I turn do that, I
hear a crack. I crane my neck, eyeing the length
of the statue. A thin fracture is shooting through
it, running from the base toward the peak, and
it suddenly hits me that—

CRASH!

chapter twenty-one

OK, *now* the entire-life-flashing-before-my-eyes thing is gonna happen. That's what I think as the chunk of statue falls on me and everything goes black.

But instead, all I see is darkness, followed by that same horrible image. The thing that I saw through the rip-tear. The embodiment of absolute horror.

I see it for longer, this time. I want to look away, but I can't. For real, it's not possible—it's just there, behind my eyelids.

And I think . . . darn it, I'm about to die, and I never even found out what that vision was. The words start to repeat in my head like a little lullaby, rocking me to sleep.

I never found out what it was. I never found out what it was. I never found out what it was.

Found!

OUT!

Words twist and shift and slide together.

"Found!" It's Quint. "Found him!" he says.
And he's talking about me. I feel rubble
shifting, falling off me.

"OUT!" It's Wracksaw, roaring, "OUT OF MY
WAY!"

I feel something crawling near my ankle. I bite
back a scream and look down, expecting it to be
the same foul rodents that piled atop Quint. But
it's not. It's a strayfur.

Specifically, it's the strayfur I slipped on. The
dead one.

Only . . . somehow it's not dead anymore. It's
moving in a herky-jerky, shuffling manner,
reminding me a bit of how Alfred walks.

And the realization hits me like a comet. This
strayfur isn't dead. It's *undead.*

It was bitten by Stargrove. Stargrove is a
zombie monster. And zombies make more
zombies. Which means this entire place . . . is
now filled with hundreds of zombified strayfurs.

And this is terrifying . . . unless you know
how to control hundreds of zombies.

I think back to Ghazt's words: *Now you are the
general, Jack.*

Until this moment, I never truly considered what it would mean to wield the powers once wielded by Ghazt.

Ghazt is evil. Ghazt served Ṛeżżőcħ. Ghazt helped me solely out of desire for revenge against Thrull. Ghazt, in the end, was weakened and broken. But that was only because of the error that occurred when Evie tried to summon him to my world—the error that caused his true, godlike form to be replaced by a ridiculous monstrosity.

So now . . . I'm supposed to take on that mantle? Use those powers? If I do, I'm crossing a bridge that can't be uncrossed.

How far will I go to stop Ṛeżżőcħ and to save my dimension and my friends?

Dumb question, Jack. I'll go as far as I need to.

But what if in doing that . . . I lose control?

Thrull weighs heavy on me. And not just the massive stone chunk of his head currently sitting atop my body. It's the information we've learned about Thrull that presses down on me— knowing that, at one point, he was *not* pure evil. He fought against the servants of Ṛeżżőcħ. His greatest moment was right here—on this ground where I'm now lying.

How did he turn evil? Did he make a choice? Or did it just . . . happen?

Could it happen to anyone?

At the forbidden fortress, I saw June about to be killed—and the Cosmic Hand saw, too. It acted on its own, to save her. And that terrified me. It meant I was no longer fully in control of the hand, or of myself. And if I'm not fully in control of myself, I can't be fully in control of what I become.

That was the most frightening part.

But Dave saw my fear, understood it, and told me to lean into it. Accept and trust it would work out. And I've been trying. I've been trying so, so hard. Accepting, continuing to power forward even as this hideous, otherworldly force was becoming stranger, larger, more a *part of me.*

But knowing what I now know about Thrull? Can I keep trusting what I'm doing is right, when there's no way to truly know?

Light splashes my face.

The world comes into focus—I see a chunk of rubble being lifted off me.

Wracksaw looms over me. I stare up at him— and pain rips through my arm. The Cosmic Hand twitches.

But I fight it. I still have the faintest mental grip on the power of the Cosmic Hand. It's a bucking bronco and I'm riding it, trying to hold on.

Two more zombie strayfurs limp into my field of vision. One tries to fly, like it hasn't realized it's dead. It leaves the ground for a moment, then falls.

My eyes flick up. Wracksaw doesn't notice the strayfurs. I have the memory of his voice in the back of my mind. I shut my eyes, and I see him . . .

THIS LABORATORY IS WHERE I BUILD MONSTERS. BUT YOU WON'T NEED TO BE BUILT. YOU ARE WELL ON YOUR WAY TO BECOMING A MONSTROSITY YOURSELF—WITHOUT MY HELP.

My eyes reopen. And now . . . my vision is filled with a thousand mind-doodles.

I'm seeing the thoughts of the strayfurs. Which means it's not only Stargrove I can communicate with and command. And if I can control every strayfur here, then I'll know for sure: if I get home, I can control every zombie marching toward the Tower.

I feel the hand growing around me again, forming the Slicer, the midnight blade, jagged and fleshy and made of the same strange skin that covered the Scrapken's body. I stop fighting it. And I deliver the mind-doodle: get this statue off of me.

At once, the zombie strayfurs swarm toward me, turning the world black as they dive beneath the monument, pushing, nudging, beaks digging into the ground and chipping at the stone.

The statue starts to move, just slightly.

Enough for me to get one leg free.

Wracksaw staggers back.

"Wracksaw!" I shout, sitting up. "Didn't you realize? Didn't your all-knowing, brilliant mind consider? That if the hand wrestled control of my being, took over—then *your enemy would be a monster*?"

At once, the undead strayfurs pull the monument up, freeing me completely.

I stand.

The strayfurs swirl, forming a tornado around me. A massive, terrible army of the undead.

I am the general that Ghazt said I was. Which means I am the general that an *evil god* wanted me to be.

I gaze out at the Last Hurrah's destruction. The Thrull statue half-smashed, the other a heap of rubble.

I see Globlet and Seabiscuit. And I see Quint, free from the rodents. Clothes torn, bits of gnawed fabric waving gently in the breeze, covered in tiny bits of rubble—but alive and OK.

And for a split second, I think I see fear on his face. But no.

What I see on his face—it's belief.

Belief in *me*.

Not everyone gets to have that. I didn't. Not until the world ended. Now here I am, controlling an army of the undead. And I see belief on my friend's face.

June, Dirk, I think. *I hope you guys are OK. Because Quint and I are just about ready to come on home.* A quick conversation with Shuggoth. And then we're done here.

Wracksaw calls to the strayfurs, ordering them to attack me. Shouting at them until his cries turn to begging and then, finally, he simply stares at the buzzing horde. Then he looks at me with hate in his eyes—but something else, too. Fear. And wonder. "Who do you think you are—?" he starts, then goes quiet.

The buzzing above us grows louder. A swirling mass of zombified creatures, some barely able to fly, but still aloft, staying in the air because I command them to.

"But, soon, Wracksaw," I say, "I'm going to find out . . ."

And then I send the undead creatures, all at once, a tremendous swarm—straight at Wracksaw . . .

Acknowledgments

A huge thanks to so many awesome people! Doug Holgate, DUH, for everything. Leila Sales and Dana Leydig: I'm pretty sure I now owe you both a life debt—you're incredible. As always, I'm in Jim Hoover's debt for the perfecto cover design and for another impeccable, immaculate, inspired interior. Ken Wright, you have guided and steered every single Last Kids book—and always with kindness, consideration, and care. I've been so very lucky, and now my luck continues; a giant cheers and a giant thank-you to Tamar Brazis—I can't wait for all that's to come. I'm tremendously grateful for the work of so many: Debra Polansky, Joe English, Todd Jones, Mary McGrath, Abigail Powers, Krista Ahlberg, Marinda Valenti, Sola Akinlana, Sarah Chassé, Gaby Corzo, Ginny Dominguez, Emily Romero, Elyse Marshall, Carmela Iaria, Christina Colangelo, Felicity Vallence, Sarah Moses, Alex Garber, Lauren Festa, Michael Hetrick, Trevor Ingerson, Kim Ryan, Helen Boomer, and everyone in PYR Sales and PYR Audio. Hugely appreciative, as always, of Dan Lazar, Cecilia de la Campa, Alessandra Birch, Torie Doherty-Munro, and everyone at Writers House. Giant-sized hugs to Josh Pruett, Haley Mancini, and Mike Mandolese. And the biggest thanks of all to my wife, Alyse, for cheering me on and bearing with me and keeping me afloat.

MAX BRALLIER!

is a #1 *New York Times*, *USA Today*, and *Wall Street Journal* bestselling author. His books and series include The Last Kids on Earth, Eerie Elementary, Mister Shivers, Galactic Hot Dogs, and *Can YOU Survive the Zombie Apocalypse?* He is a writer and executive producer for Netflix's Emmy Award–winning adaptation of The Last Kids on Earth.

DOUGLAS HOLGATE!

is the illustrator of the #1 *New York Times* bestselling series The Last Kids on Earth from Viking (now also an Emmy-winning Netflix animated series) and the cocreator and illustrator of the graphic novel *Clem Hetherington and the Ironwood Race* for Scholastic Graphix.

He has worked for the last twenty years making books and comics for publishers around the world from his garage in Victoria, Australia. He lives with his family and a large, fat dog that could possibly be part polar bear in the Australian bush on five acres surrounded by eighty-million-year-old volcanic boulders.

You can find his work at DouglasBotHolgate.com and on Twitter @DouglasHolgate.

JOIN TODAY!

Have your parent or guardian sign up for the official Last Kids on Earth Fan Club to receive a Welcome Kit in the mail! Plus, you'll receive exclusive Last Kids news, sneak previews, and behind-the-scenes info via our e-newsletter!

VISIT TheLastKidsonEarthClub.com
TO LEARN MORE